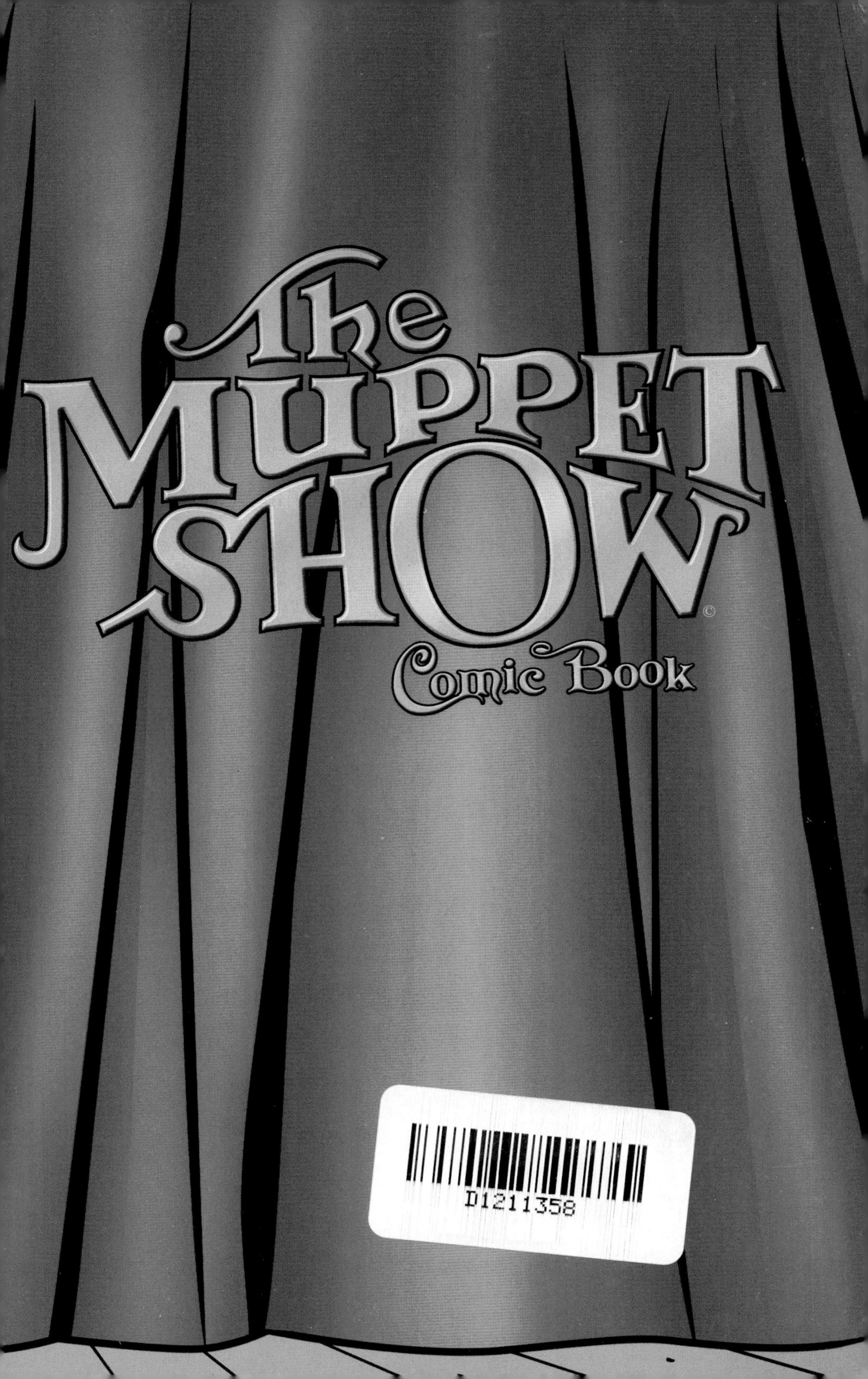
The MUPPET SHOW©
Comic Book

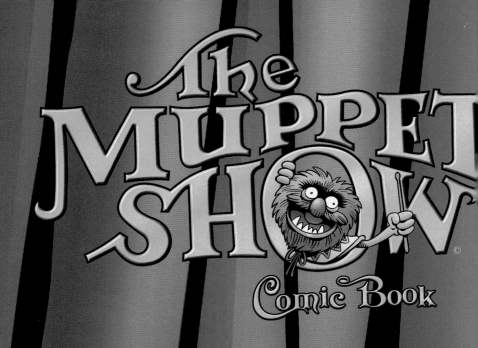

The MUPPET SHOW
Comic Book

SPECIAL THANKS: TISHANA
WILLIAMS, IVONNE FELICIANO,
AND THE MUPPETS STUDIO

AND A VERY HEARTY ROUND
OF APPLAUSE FOR DAVE
SHELTON!

MEET THE MUPPETS

WRITTEN AND DRAWN BY **Roger Langridge**

COLORS **Digikore Studios**

LETTERS **Deron Bennett**

EDITOR **Paul Morrissey**

COVERS **Roger Langridge**

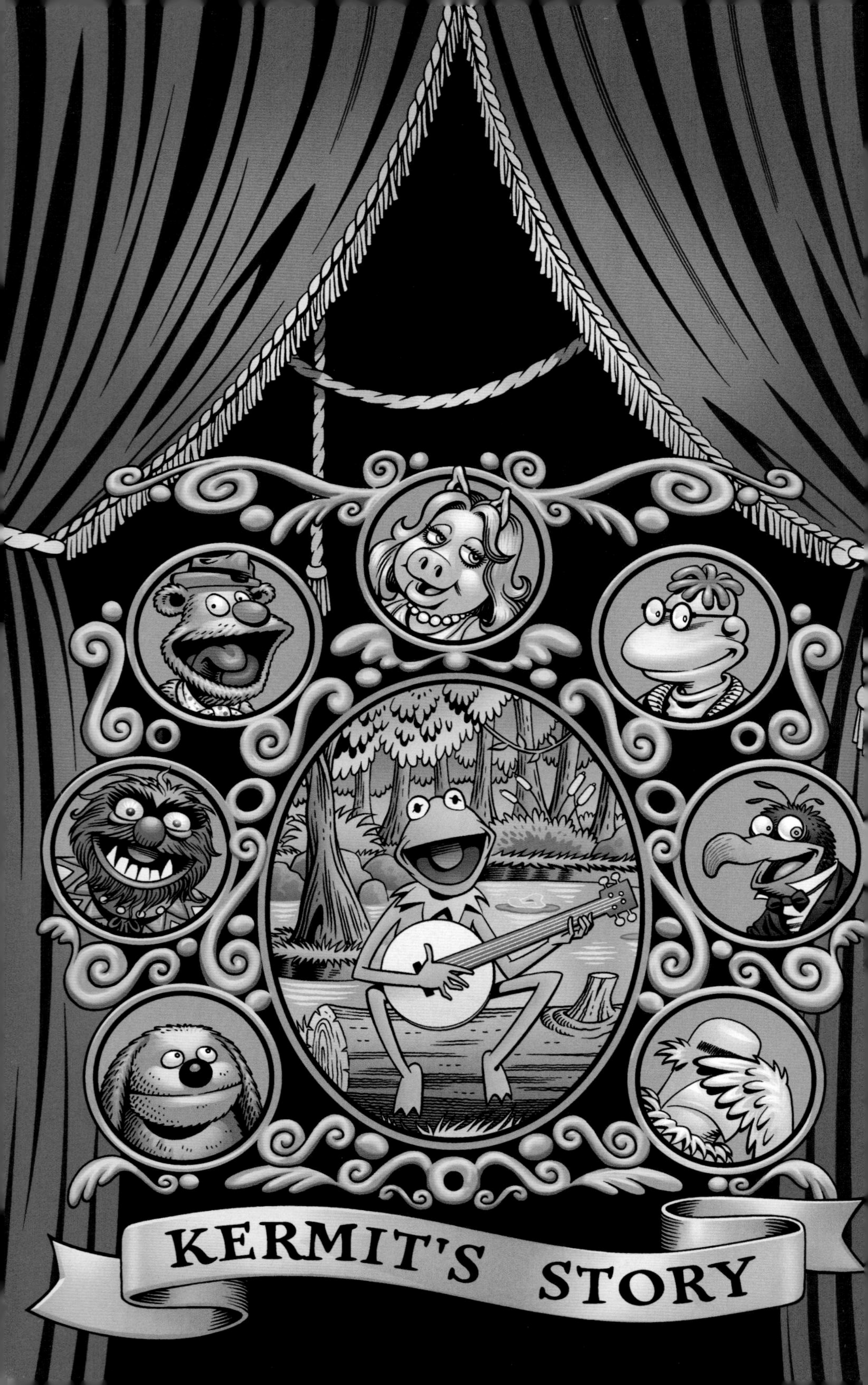
KERMIT'S STORY

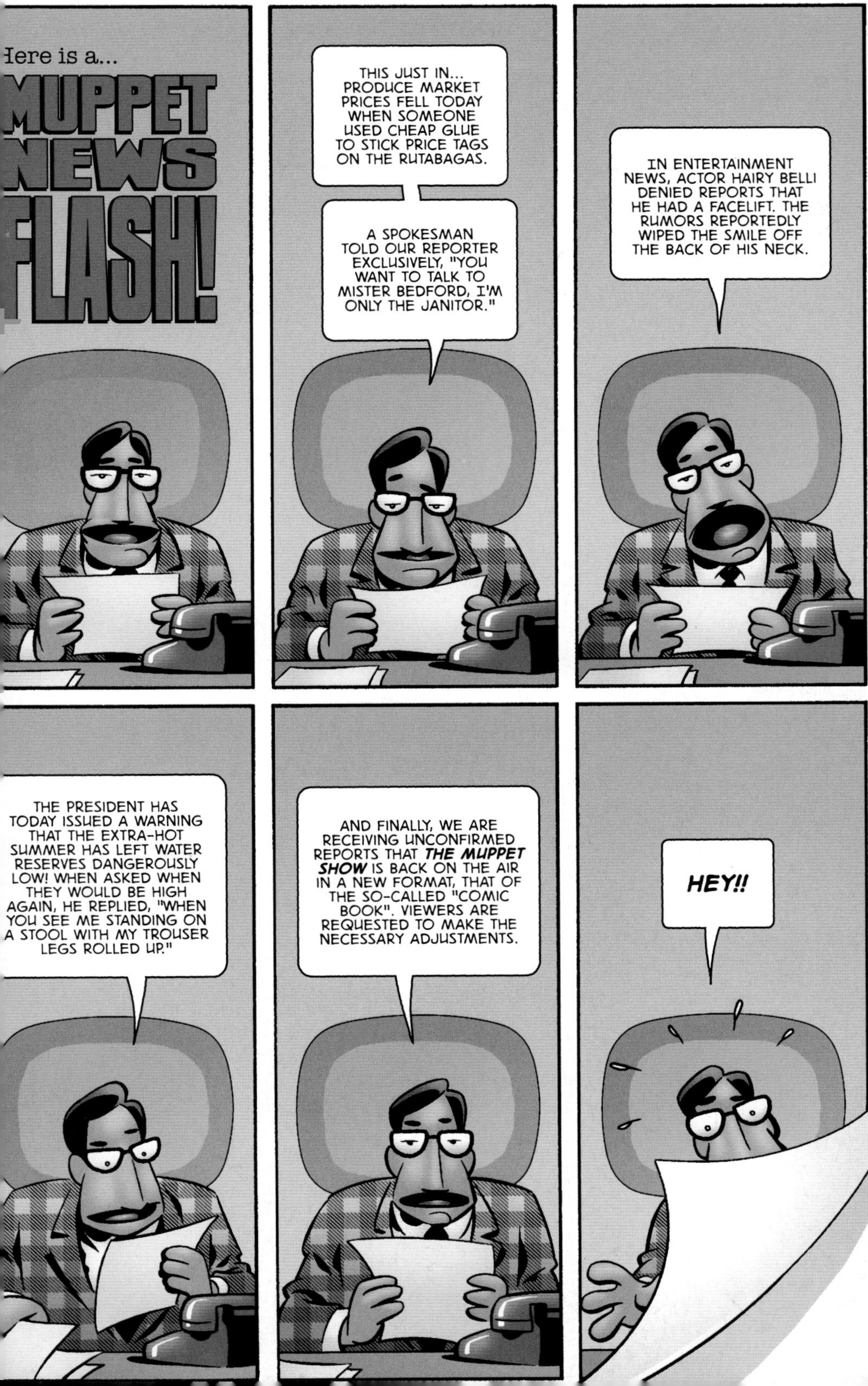
Here is a...
MUPPET NEWS FLASH!
THIS JUST IN... PRODUCE MARKET PRICES FELL TODAY WHEN SOMEONE USED CHEAP GLUE TO STICK PRICE TAGS ON THE RUTABAGAS.
A SPOKESMAN TOLD OUR REPORTER EXCLUSIVELY, "YOU WANT TO TALK TO MISTER BEDFORD, I'M ONLY THE JANITOR."
IN ENTERTAINMENT NEWS, ACTOR HAIRY BELLI DENIED REPORTS THAT HE HAD A FACELIFT. THE RUMORS REPORTEDLY WIPED THE SMILE OFF THE BACK OF HIS NECK.
THE PRESIDENT HAS TODAY ISSUED A WARNING THAT THE EXTRA-HOT SUMMER HAS LEFT WATER RESERVES DANGEROUSLY LOW! WHEN ASKED WHEN THEY WOULD BE HIGH AGAIN, HE REPLIED, "WHEN YOU SEE ME STANDING ON A STOOL WITH MY TROUSER LEGS ROLLED UP."
AND FINALLY, WE ARE RECEIVING UNCONFIRMED REPORTS THAT ***THE MUPPET SHOW*** IS BACK ON THE AIR IN A NEW FORMAT, THAT OF THE SO-CALLED "COMIC BOOK". VIEWERS ARE REQUESTED TO MAKE THE NECESSARY ADJUSTMENTS.
HEY!!

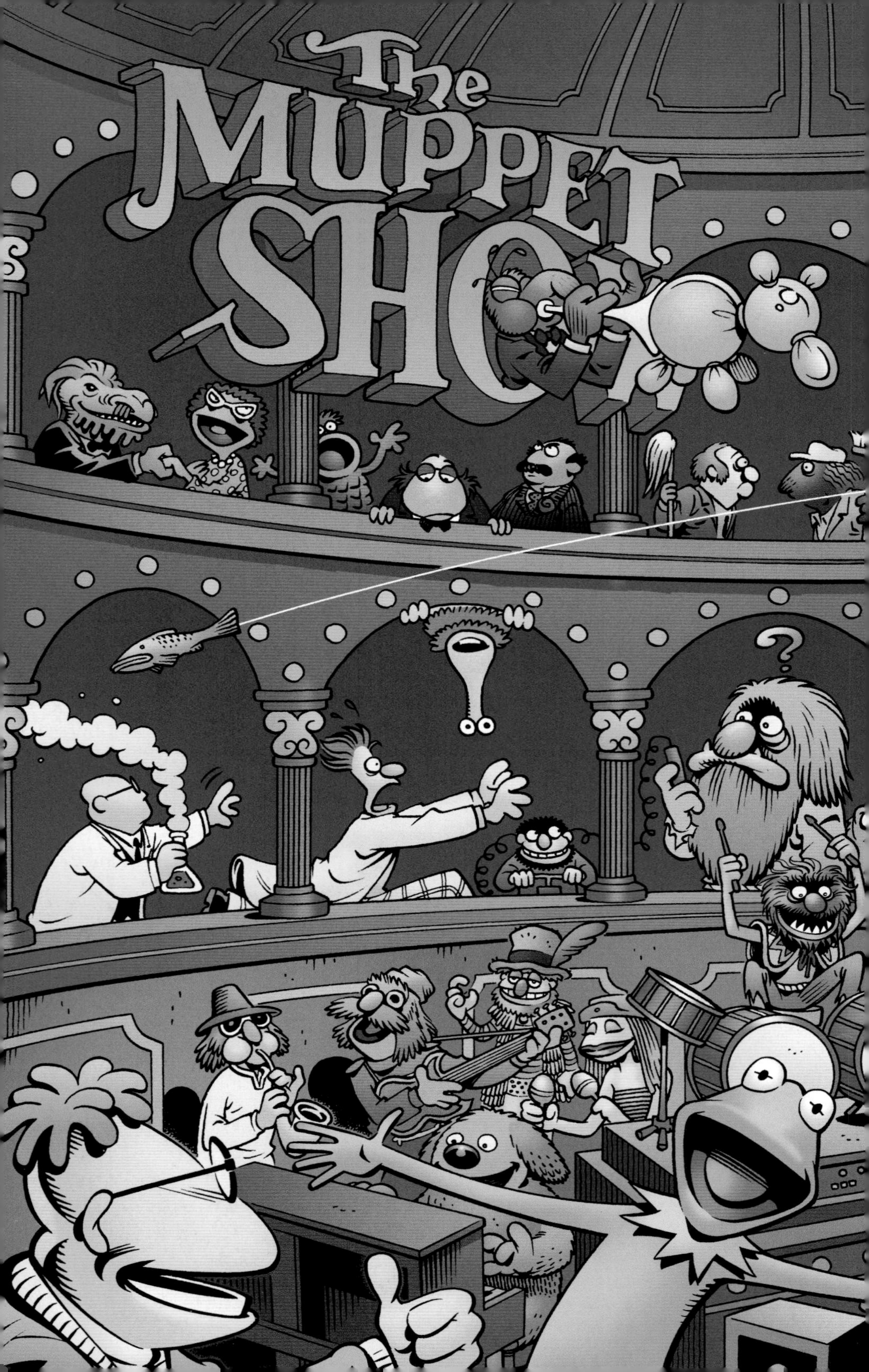
The
MUPPET
SHO

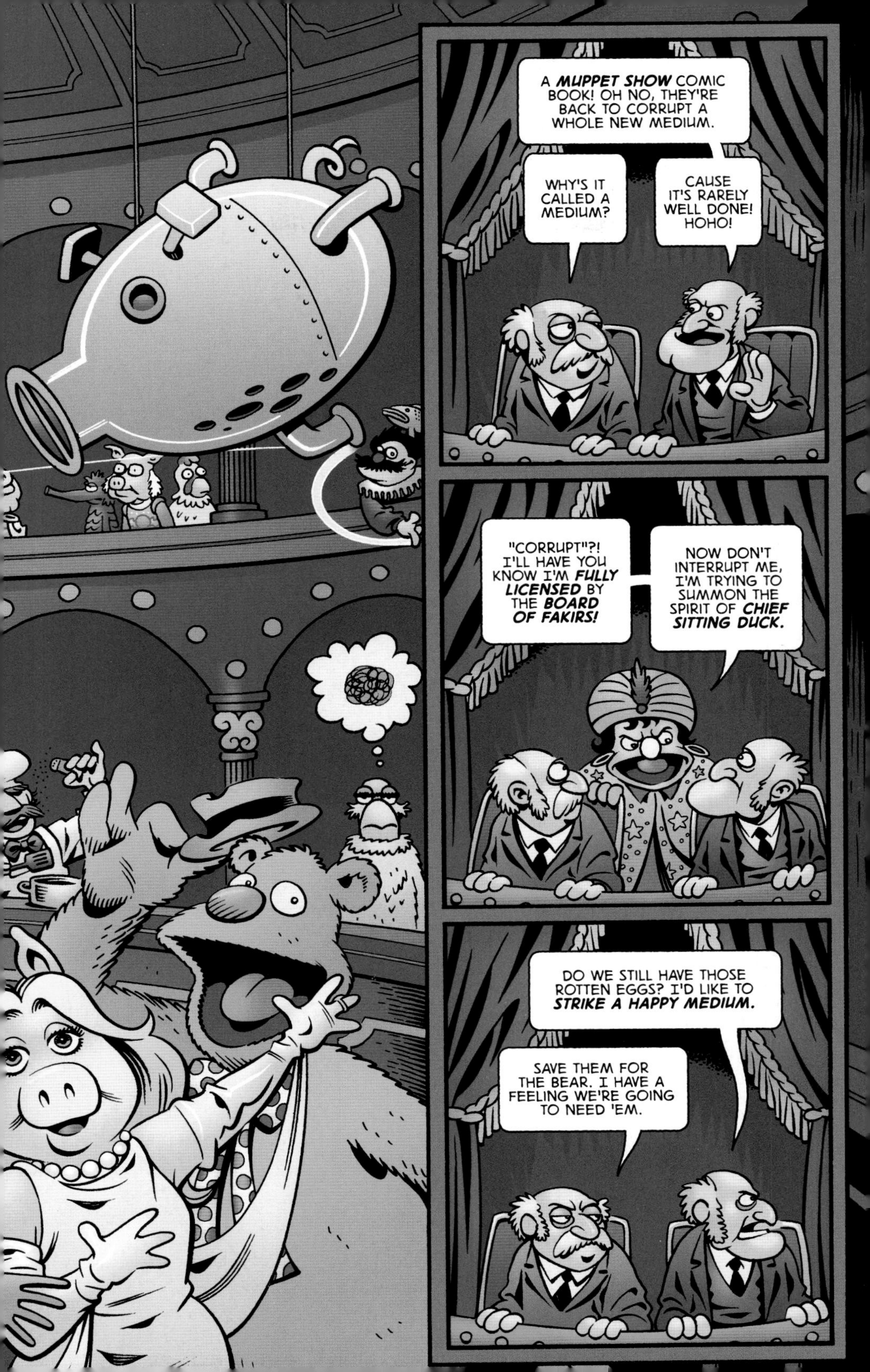
A MUPPET SHOW COMIC BOOK! OH NO, THEY'RE BACK TO CORRUPT A WHOLE NEW MEDIUM.
WHY'S IT CALLED A MEDIUM?
CAUSE IT'S RARELY WELL DONE! HOHO!
"CORRUPT"?! I'LL HAVE YOU KNOW I'M FULLY LICENSED BY THE BOARD OF FAKIRS!
NOW DON'T INTERRUPT ME, I'M TRYING TO SUMMON THE SPIRIT OF CHIEF SITTING DUCK.
DO WE STILL HAVE THOSE ROTTEN EGGS? I'D LIKE TO STRIKE A HAPPY MEDIUM.
SAVE THEM FOR THE BEAR. I HAVE A FEELING WE'RE GOING TO NEED 'EM.

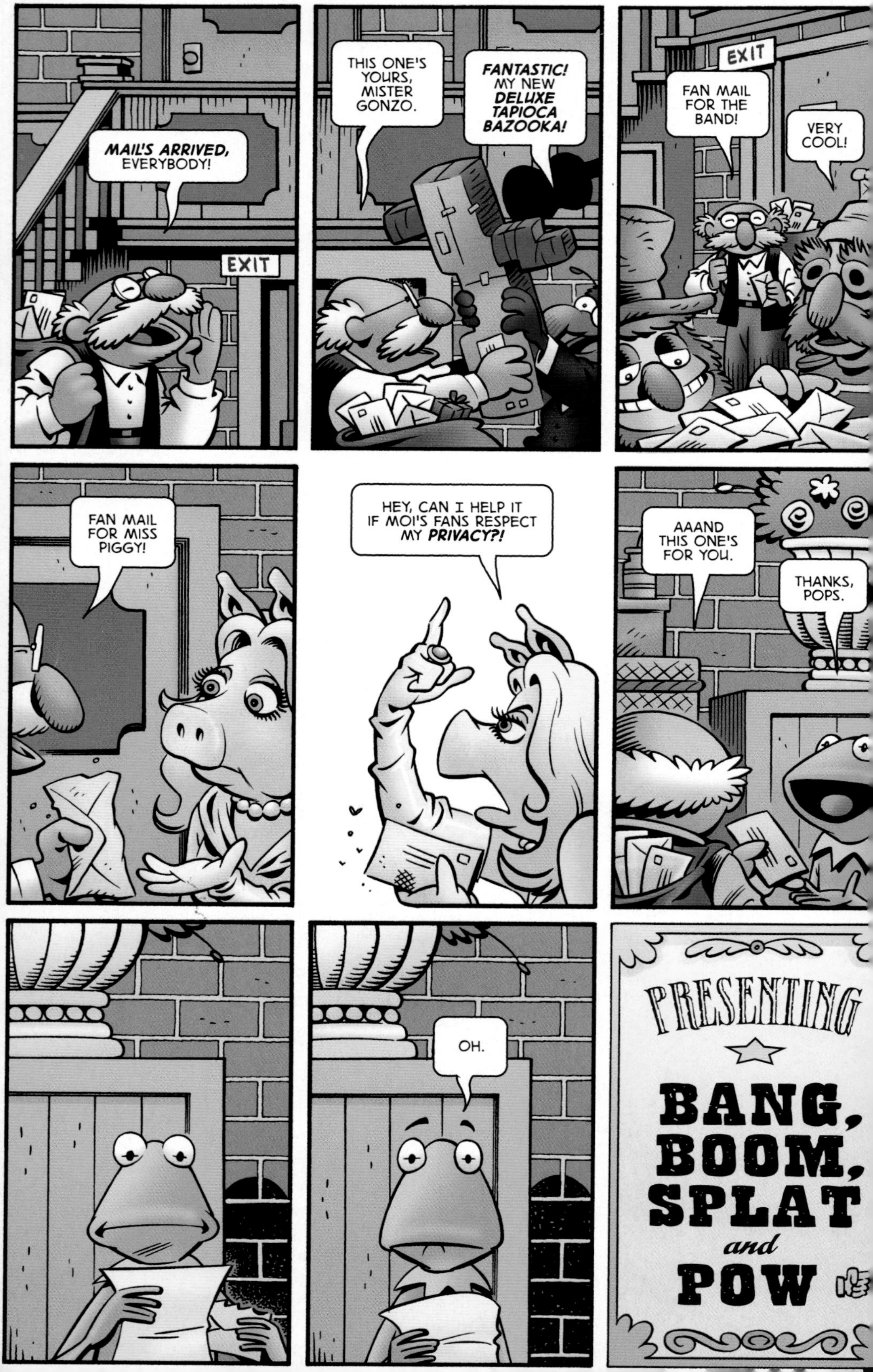
MAIL'S ARRIVED, EVERYBODY!
EXIT
THIS ONE'S YOURS, MISTER GONZO.
FANTASTIC! MY NEW DELUXE TAPIOCA BAZOOKA!
EXIT
FAN MAIL FOR THE BAND!
VERY COOL!
FAN MAIL FOR MISS PIGGY!
HEY, CAN I HELP IT IF MOI'S FANS RESPECT MY PRIVACY?!
AAAND THIS ONE'S FOR YOU.
THANKS, POPS.
OH.
PRESENTING
BANG, BOOM, SPLAT and POW

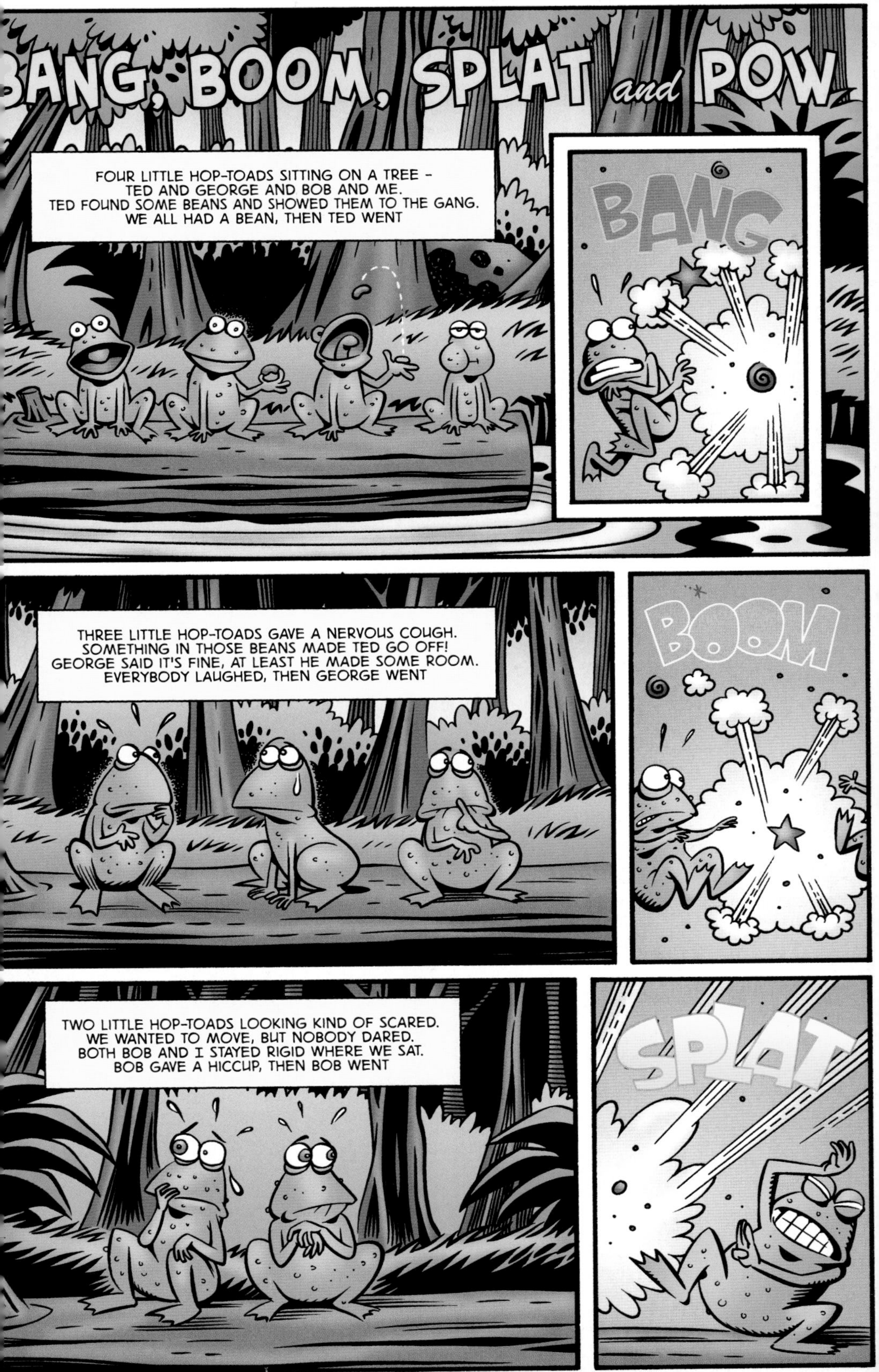
BANG, BOOM, SPLAT and POW
FOUR LITTLE HOP-TOADS SITTING ON A TREE - TED AND GEORGE AND BOB AND ME. TED FOUND SOME BEANS AND SHOWED THEM TO THE GANG. WE ALL HAD A BEAN, THEN TED WENT
BANG
THREE LITTLE HOP-TOADS GAVE A NERVOUS COUGH. SOMETHING IN THOSE BEANS MADE TED GO OFF! GEORGE SAID IT'S FINE, AT LEAST HE MADE SOME ROOM. EVERYBODY LAUGHED, THEN GEORGE WENT
BOOM
TWO LITTLE HOP-TOADS LOOKING KIND OF SCARED. WE WANTED TO MOVE, BUT NOBODY DARED. BOTH BOB AND I STAYED RIGID WHERE WE SAT. BOB GAVE A HICCUP, THEN BOB WENT
SPLAT

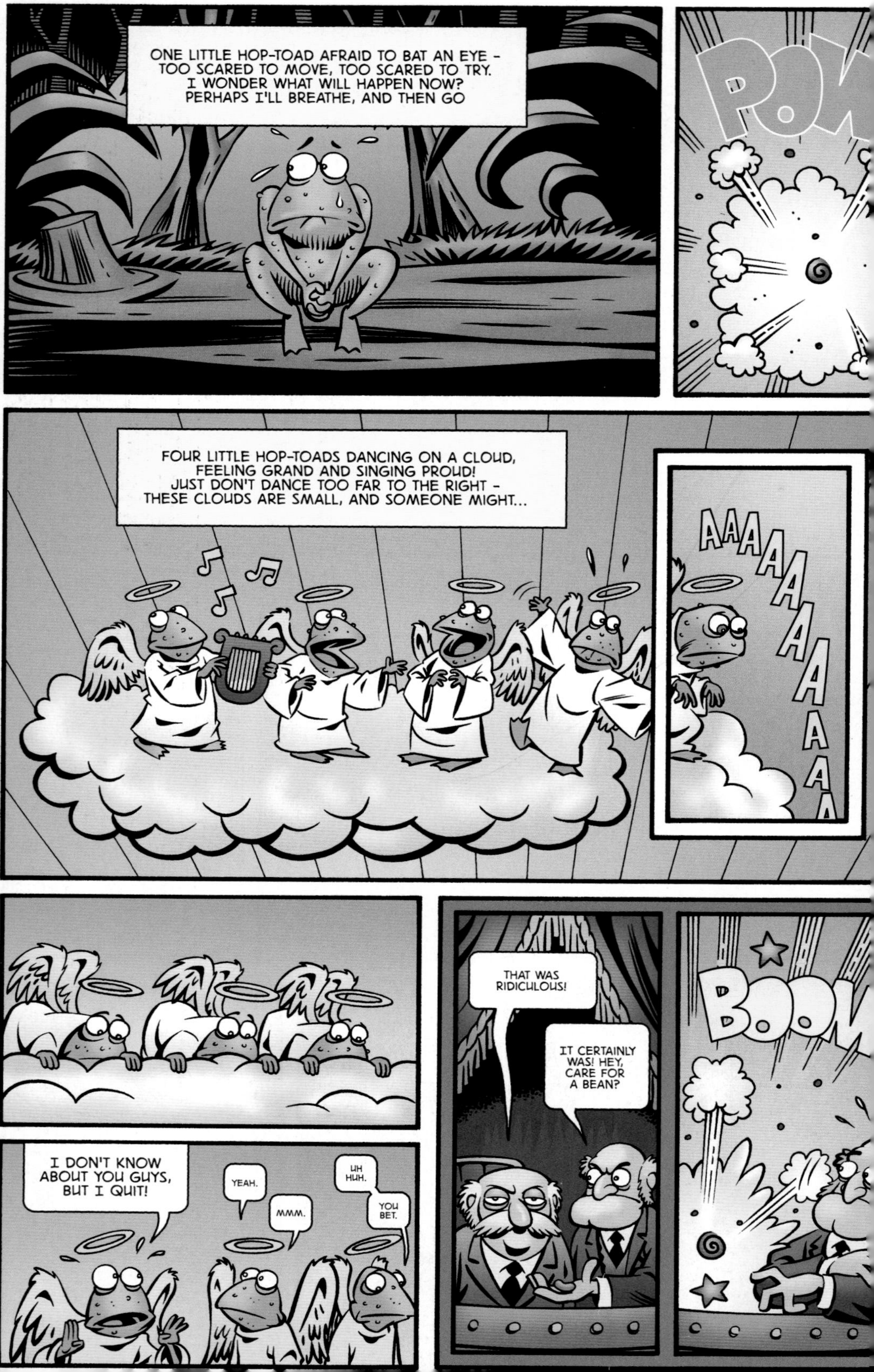

ONE LITTLE HOP-TOAD AFRAID TO BAT AN EYE - TOO SCARED TO MOVE, TOO SCARED TO TRY. I WONDER WHAT WILL HAPPEN NOW? PERHAPS I'LL BREATHE, AND THEN GO
FOUR LITTLE HOP-TOADS DANCING ON A CLOUD, FEELING GRAND AND SINGING PROUD! JUST DON'T DANCE TOO FAR TO THE RIGHT - THESE CLOUDS ARE SMALL, AND SOMEONE MIGHT...
AAAAAAAAAAAA
I DON'T KNOW ABOUT YOU GUYS, BUT I QUIT!
YEAH.
MMM.
UH HUH.
YOU BET.
THAT WAS RIDICULOUS!
IT CERTAINLY WAS! HEY, CARE FOR A BEAN?

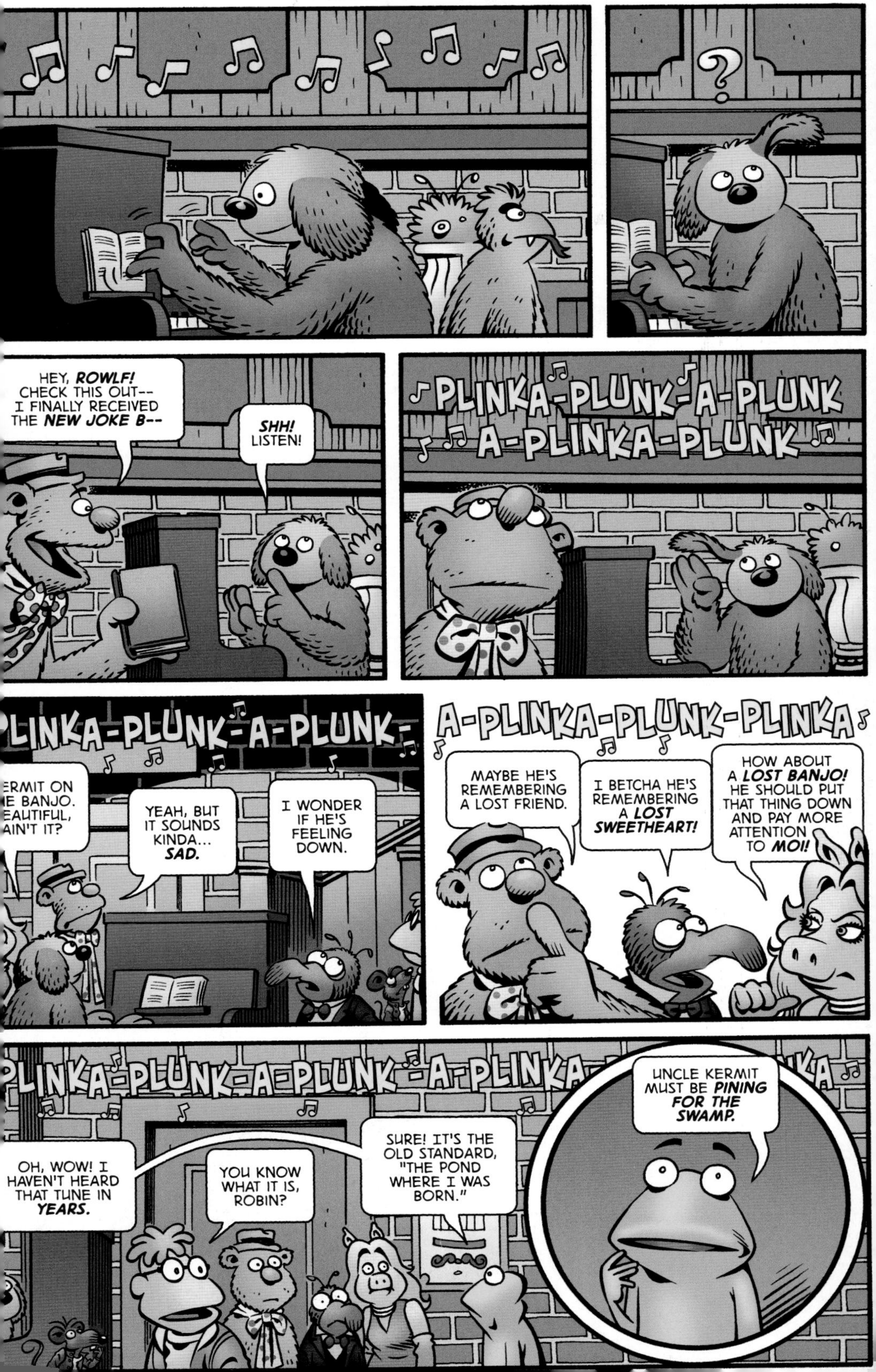

HEY, ROWLF! CHECK THIS OUT-- I FINALLY RECEIVED THE NEW JOKE B--
SHH! LISTEN!
PLINKA-PLUNK-A-PLUNK A-PLINKA-PLUNK
PLINKA-PLUNK-A-PLUNK
ERMIT ON E BANJO. EAUTIFUL, AIN'T IT?
YEAH, BUT IT SOUNDS KINDA... SAD.
I WONDER IF HE'S FEELING DOWN.
A-PLINKA-PLUNK-PLINKA
MAYBE HE'S REMEMBERING A LOST FRIEND.
I BETCHA HE'S REMEMBERING A LOST SWEETHEART!
HOW ABOUT A LOST BANJO! HE SHOULD PUT THAT THING DOWN AND PAY MORE ATTENTION TO MOI!
PLINKA-PLUNK-A-PLUNK-A-PLINKA
OH, WOW! I HAVEN'T HEARD THAT TUNE IN YEARS.
YOU KNOW WHAT IT IS, ROBIN?
SURE! IT'S THE OLD STANDARD, "THE POND WHERE I WAS BORN."
UNCLE KERMIT MUST BE PINING FOR THE SWAMP.

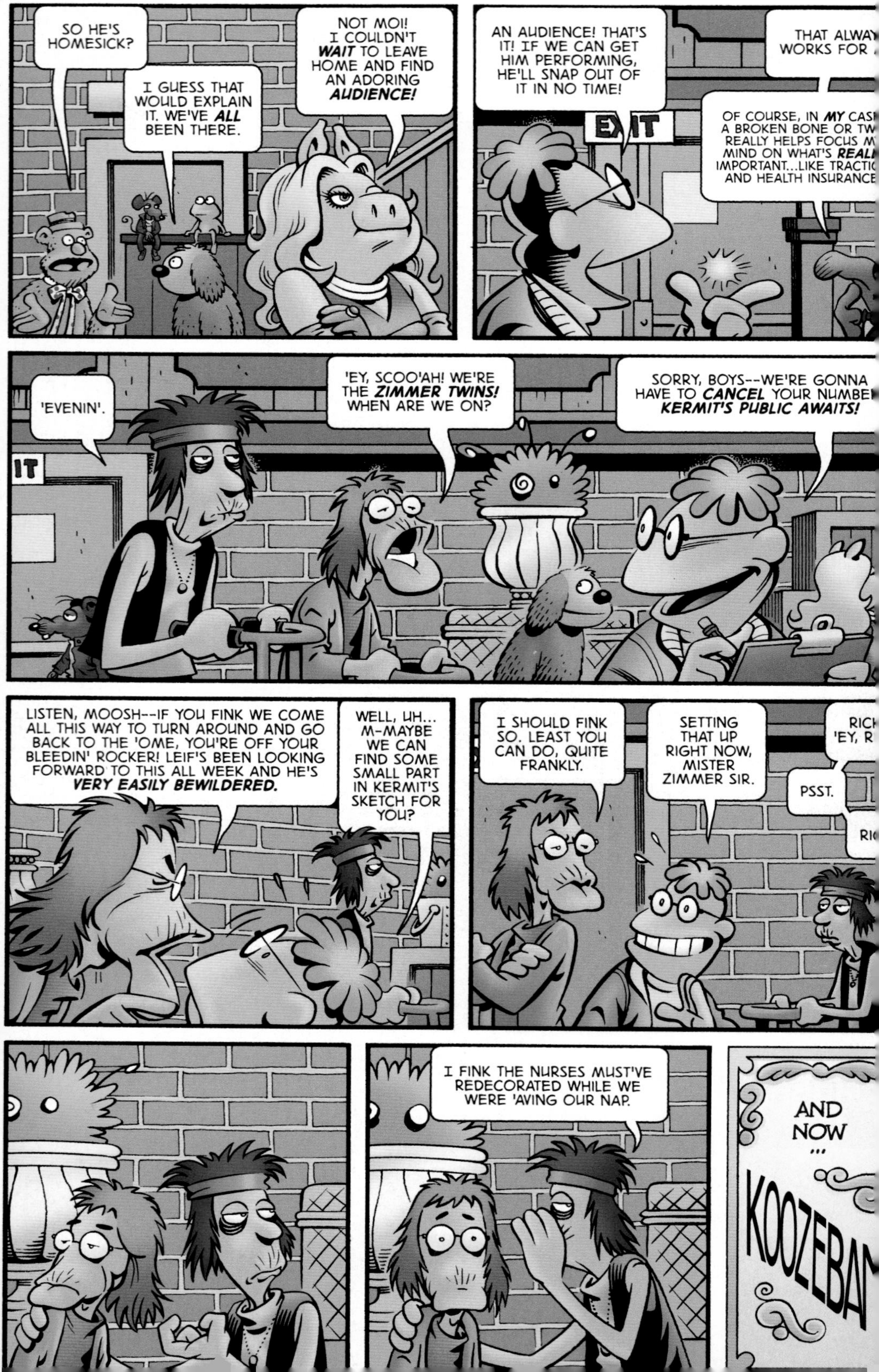
SO HE'S HOMESICK?
I GUESS THAT WOULD EXPLAIN IT. WE'VE ALL BEEN THERE.
NOT MOI! I COULDN'T WAIT TO LEAVE HOME AND FIND AN ADORING AUDIENCE!
AN AUDIENCE! THAT'S IT! IF WE CAN GET HIM PERFORMING, HE'LL SNAP OUT OF IT IN NO TIME!
EXIT
THAT ALWAY WORKS FOR
OF COURSE, IN MY CAS A BROKEN BONE OR TW REALLY HELPS FOCUS M MIND ON WHAT'S REAL IMPORTANT...LIKE TRACTI AND HEALTH INSURANCE
'EVENIN'.
'EY, SCOO'AH! WE'RE THE ZIMMER TWINS! WHEN ARE WE ON?
SORRY, BOYS--WE'RE GONNA HAVE TO CANCEL YOUR NUMBE KERMIT'S PUBLIC AWAITS!
LISTEN, MOOSH--IF YOU FINK WE COME ALL THIS WAY TO TURN AROUND AND GO BACK TO THE 'OME, YOU'RE OFF YOUR BLEEDIN' ROCKER! LEIF'S BEEN LOOKING FORWARD TO THIS ALL WEEK AND HE'S VERY EASILY BEWILDERED.
WELL, UH... M-MAYBE WE CAN FIND SOME SMALL PART IN KERMIT'S SKETCH FOR YOU?
I SHOULD FINK SO. LEAST YOU CAN DO, QUITE FRANKLY.
SETTING THAT UP RIGHT NOW, MISTER ZIMMER SIR.
RIC 'EY, R
PSST.
RI
I FINK THE NURSES MUST'VE REDECORATED WHILE WE WERE 'AVING OUR NAP.
AND NOW ...
KOOZEBA

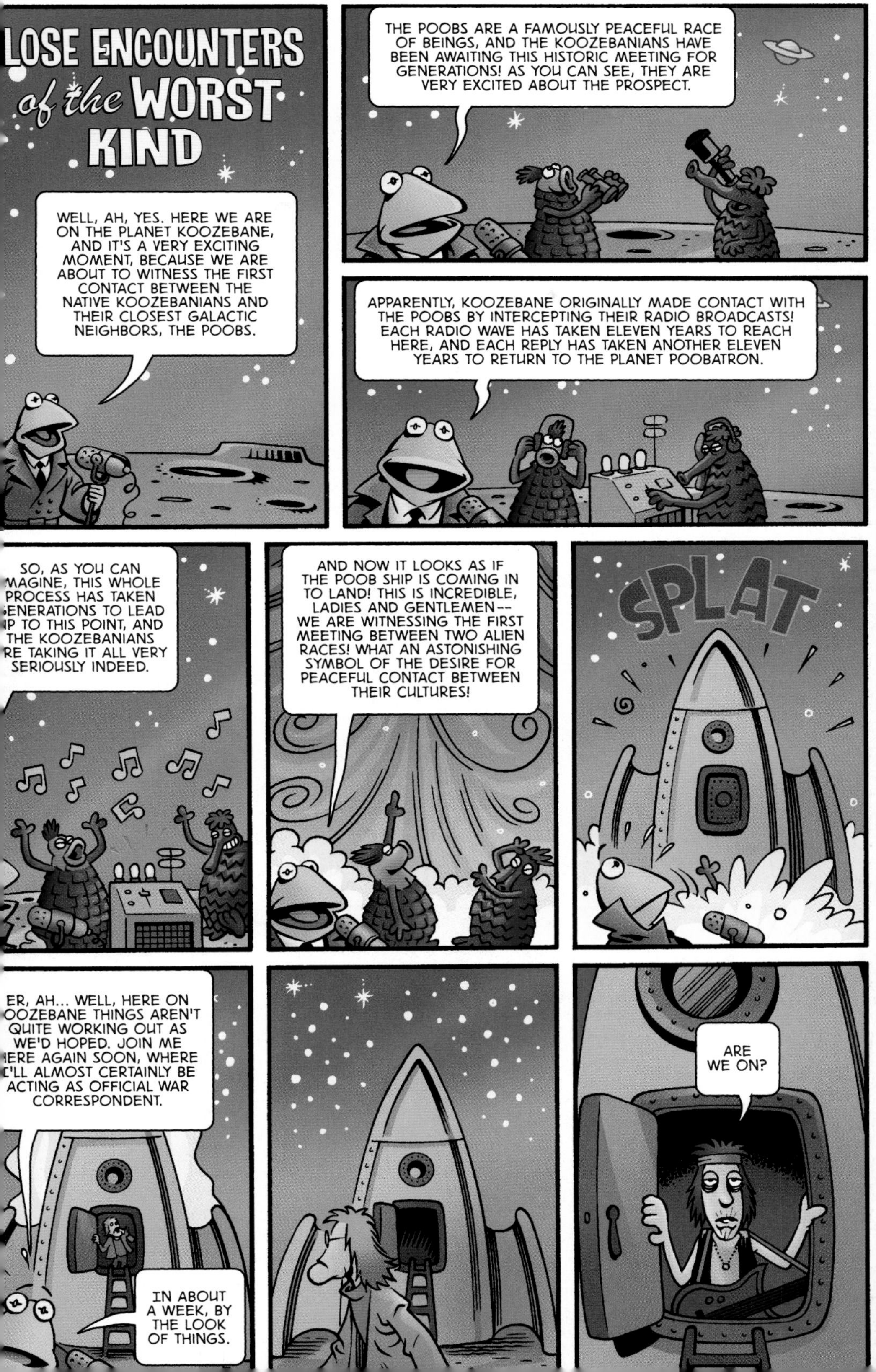
LOSE ENCOUNTERS of the WORST KIND
WELL, AH, YES. HERE WE ARE ON THE PLANET KOOZEBANE, AND IT'S A VERY EXCITING MOMENT, BECAUSE WE ARE ABOUT TO WITNESS THE FIRST CONTACT BETWEEN THE NATIVE KOOZEBANIANS AND THEIR CLOSEST GALACTIC NEIGHBORS, THE POOBS.
THE POOBS ARE A FAMOUSLY PEACEFUL RACE OF BEINGS, AND THE KOOZEBANIANS HAVE BEEN AWAITING THIS HISTORIC MEETING FOR GENERATIONS! AS YOU CAN SEE, THEY ARE VERY EXCITED ABOUT THE PROSPECT.
APPARENTLY, KOOZEBANE ORIGINALLY MADE CONTACT WITH THE POOBS BY INTERCEPTING THEIR RADIO BROADCASTS! EACH RADIO WAVE HAS TAKEN ELEVEN YEARS TO REACH HERE, AND EACH REPLY HAS TAKEN ANOTHER ELEVEN YEARS TO RETURN TO THE PLANET POOBATRON.
SO, AS YOU CAN MAGINE, THIS WHOLE PROCESS HAS TAKEN ENERATIONS TO LEAD P TO THIS POINT, AND THE KOOZEBANIANS RE TAKING IT ALL VERY SERIOUSLY INDEED.
AND NOW IT LOOKS AS IF THE POOB SHIP IS COMING IN TO LAND! THIS IS INCREDIBLE, LADIES AND GENTLEMEN-- WE ARE WITNESSING THE FIRST MEETING BETWEEN TWO ALIEN RACES! WHAT AN ASTONISHING SYMBOL OF THE DESIRE FOR PEACEFUL CONTACT BETWEEN THEIR CULTURES!
SPLAT
ER, AH... WELL, HERE ON OOZEBANE THINGS AREN'T QUITE WORKING OUT AS WE'D HOPED. JOIN ME ERE AGAIN SOON, WHERE I'LL ALMOST CERTAINLY BE ACTING AS OFFICIAL WAR CORRESPONDENT.
IN ABOUT A WEEK, BY THE LOOK OF THINGS.
ARE WE ON?

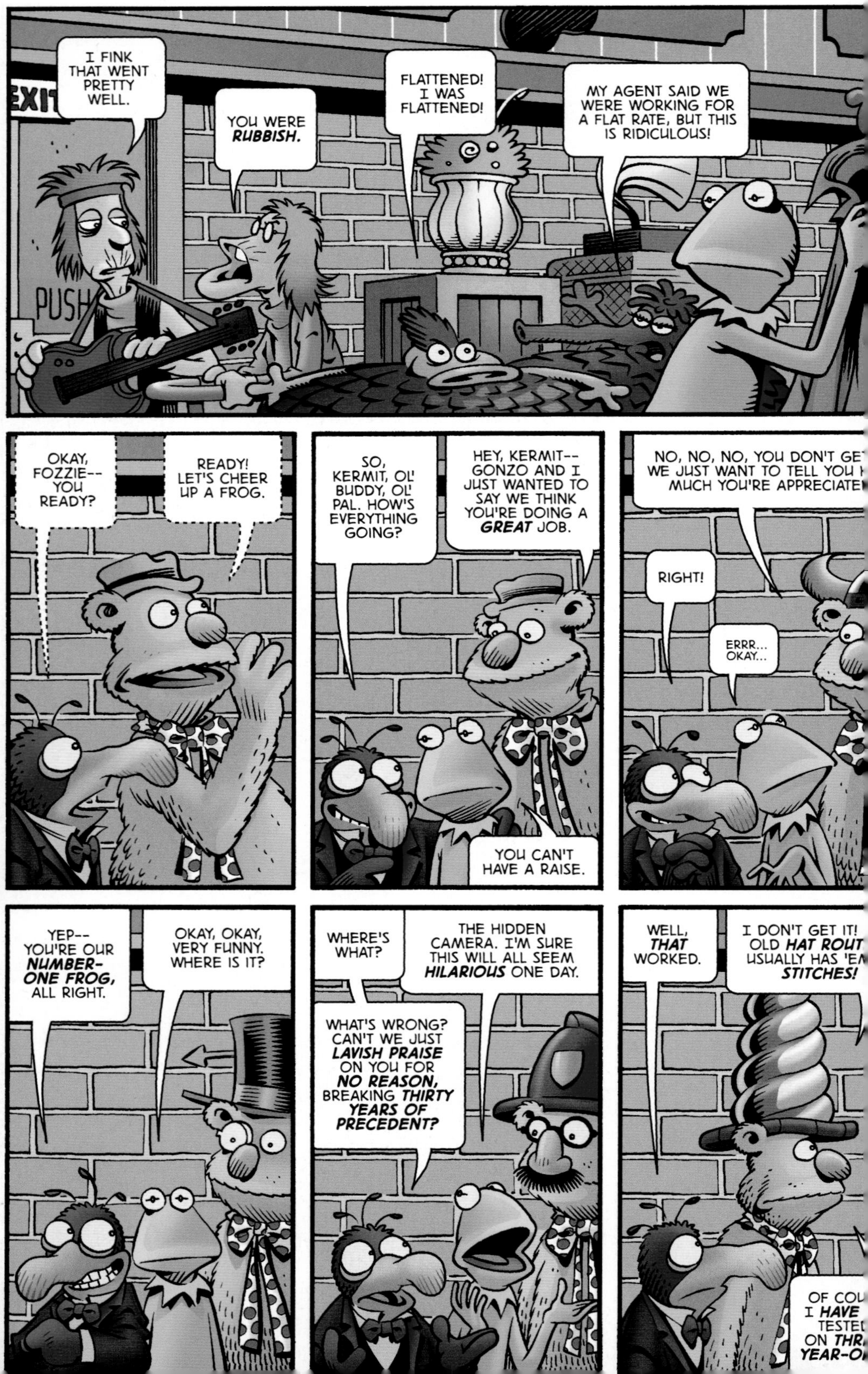

EXIT
PUSH
I FINK THAT WENT PRETTY WELL.
YOU WERE ***RUBBISH.***
FLATTENED! I WAS FLATTENED!
MY AGENT SAID WE WERE WORKING FOR A FLAT RATE, BUT THIS IS RIDICULOUS!
OKAY, FOZZIE-- YOU READY?
READY! LET'S CHEER UP A FROG.
SO, KERMIT, OL' BUDDY, OL' PAL. HOW'S EVERYTHING GOING?
HEY, KERMIT-- GONZO AND I JUST WANTED TO SAY WE THINK YOU'RE DOING A ***GREAT*** JOB.
YOU CAN'T HAVE A RAISE.
NO, NO, NO, YOU DON'T GE WE JUST WANT TO TELL YOU MUCH YOU'RE APPRECIATE
RIGHT!
ERRR... OKAY...
YEP-- YOU'RE OUR ***NUMBER-ONE FROG,*** ALL RIGHT.
OKAY, OKAY, VERY FUNNY. WHERE IS IT?
WHERE'S WHAT?
THE HIDDEN CAMERA. I'M SURE THIS WILL ALL SEEM ***HILARIOUS*** ONE DAY.
WHAT'S WRONG? CAN'T WE JUST ***LAVISH PRAISE*** ON YOU FOR ***NO REASON,*** BREAKING ***THIRTY YEARS OF PRECEDENT?***
WELL, ***THAT*** WORKED.
I DON'T GET IT! OLD ***HAT ROUT*** USUALLY HAS 'EM ***STITCHES!***
OF COU I ***HAVE*** TESTE ON ***THR YEAR-O***

GENIUS! WHEN UNCLE KERMIT TASTES THIS *LILY PAD GOULASH,* HE'LL EITHER BE *DELIGHTED* OR HE'LL REMEMBER WHY HE LEFT THE SWAMP IN THE *FIRST* PLACE!

EITHER WAY, WE'RE *GOLDEN!*

CHEF! I NEED YOUR HELP! CAN I ASK YOU TO *WHIP SOMETHING UP...?*

HØER BORSCHT DER *FAER* DER BÖERKEN...

SEE THIS ECIPE? I ED YOU TO REPARE IT OR UNCLE KERMIT.

VANTER MOE DER *CØEKER DER PÄEPER?*

NO, NO, NO... LET'S SEE, HOW CAN I MAKE THIS CLEARER?... ME WANT YOU TO COOK DISH FOR FROG! *DISH FOR FROG!* SEE?

DOEMT VIT HÖERBE KERMT *GÄSSE MØJRK SCHIX?*

GAS MARK SIX! OKAY, I THINK WE'RE GETTING SOMEWHERE. *GOULASH FOR FROGS* AT *GAS MARK SIX!*

JÄ, JÄ! *CØEKER DER FRÖEGGY-FRÖEGGY* OEURF DER *GÄSSE MØJRK SCHIX!*

ØEKER DER RÖEGGY-FRÖEGGY!

AAGH! NO, *WAIT,* YOU'RE MAKING A *TERRIBLE--*

CØEKER DER FRÖEGGY-FRÖEGGY OEURF DER *GÄSSE MØJRK SCHIX!* JÄ, JÄ!

AND NOW ...

The Swedish Chef

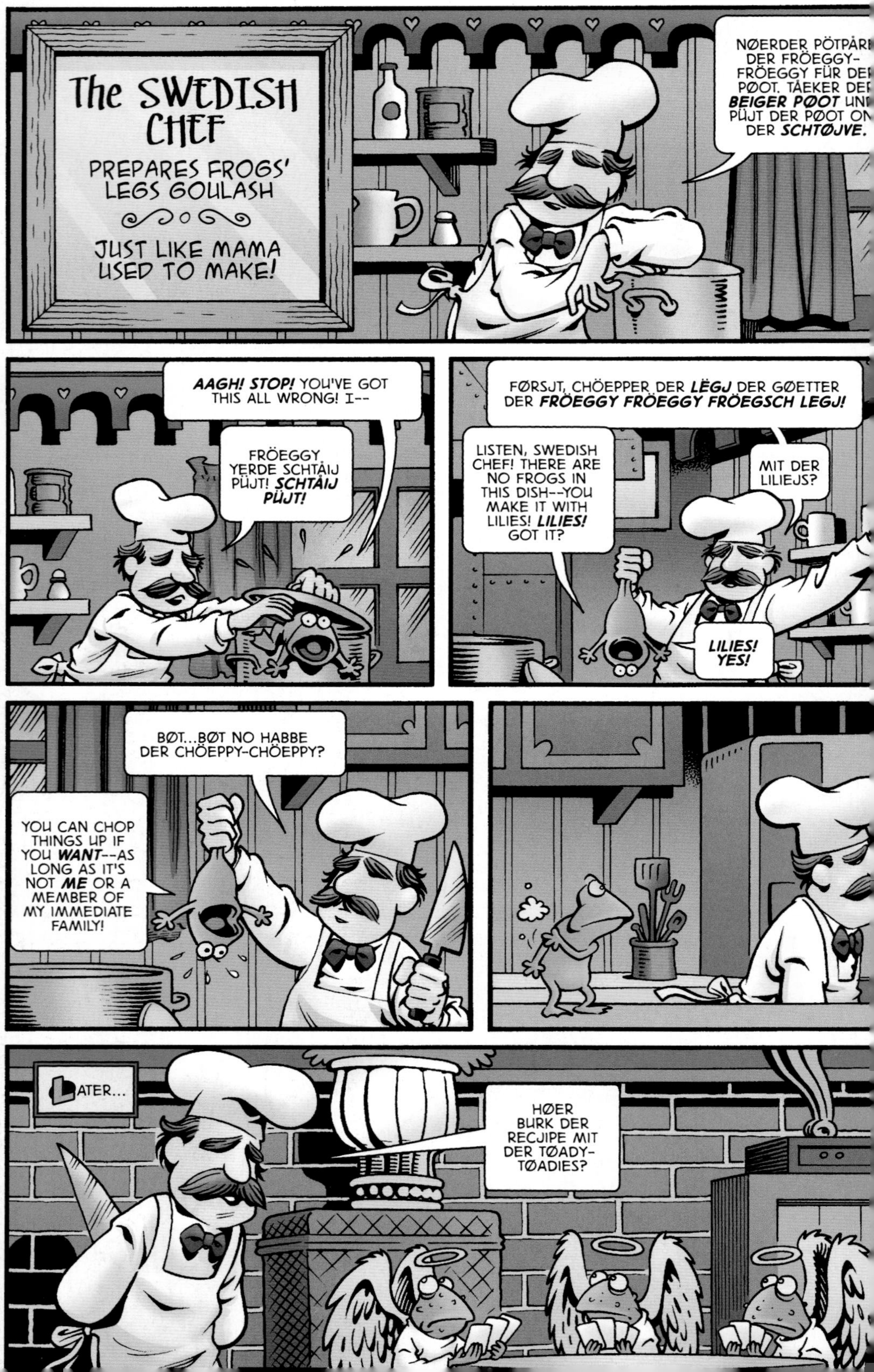
The SWEDISH CHEF
PREPARES FROGS' LEGS GOULASH
JUST LIKE MAMA USED TO MAKE!
NØERDER PÖTPÅR DER FRÖEGGY-FRÖEGGY FÜR DER PØOT. TÅEKER DER BEIGER PØOT UN PÜJT DER PØOT ON DER SCHTØJVE.
AAGH! STOP! YOU'VE GOT THIS ALL WRONG! I--
FRÖEGGY YERDE SCHTÅIJ PÜJT! SCHTÅIJ PÜJT!
FØRSJT, CHÖEPPER DER LËGJ DER GØETTER DER FRÖEGGY FRÖEGGY FRÖEGSCH LEGJ!
LISTEN, SWEDISH CHEF! THERE ARE NO FROGS IN THIS DISH--YOU MAKE IT WITH LILIES! LILIES! GOT IT?
MIT DER LILIEJS?
LILIES! YES!
BØT...BØT NO HABBE DER CHÖEPPY-CHÖEPPY?
YOU CAN CHOP THINGS UP IF YOU WANT--AS LONG AS IT'S NOT ME OR A MEMBER OF MY IMMEDIATE FAMILY!
LATER...
HØER BURK DER RECJIPE MIT DER TØADY-TØADIES?

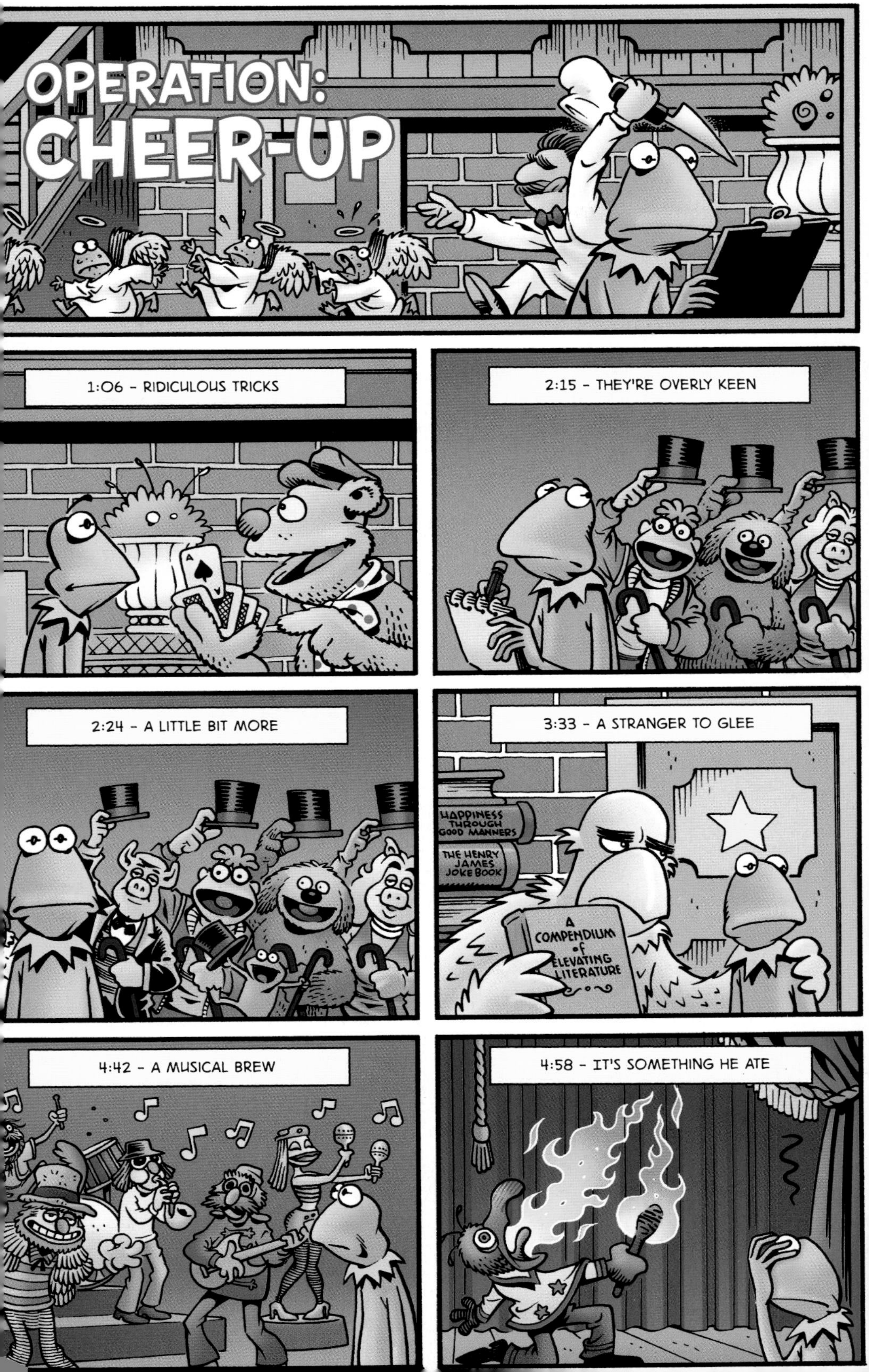
OPERATION: CHEER-UP
1:06 - RIDICULOUS TRICKS
2:15 - THEY'RE OVERLY KEEN
2:24 - A LITTLE BIT MORE
3:33 - A STRANGER TO GLEE
HAPPINESS THROUGH GOOD MANNERS
THE HENRY JAMES JOKE BOOK
A COMPENDIUM of ELEVATING LITERATURE
4:42 - A MUSICAL BREW
4:58 - IT'S SOMETHING HE ATE

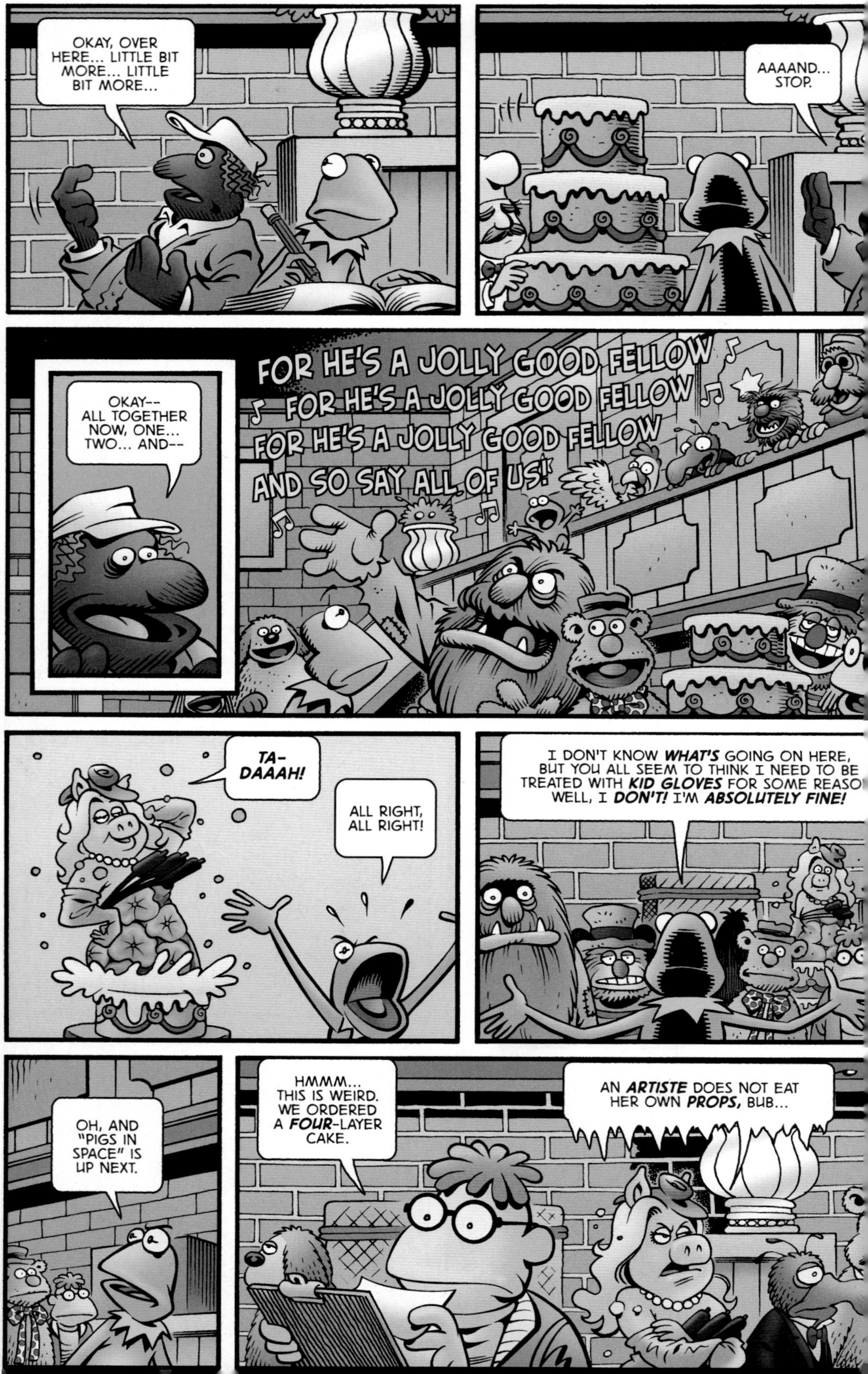

OKAY, OVER HERE... LITTLE BIT MORE... LITTLE BIT MORE...
AAAAND... STOP.
OKAY-- ALL TOGETHER NOW, ONE... TWO... AND--
FOR HE'S A JOLLY GOOD FELLOW
FOR HE'S A JOLLY GOOD FELLOW
FOR HE'S A JOLLY GOOD FELLOW
AND SO SAY ALL OF US!
TA-DAAAH!
ALL RIGHT, ALL RIGHT!
I DON'T KNOW WHAT'S GOING ON HERE, BUT YOU ALL SEEM TO THINK I NEED TO BE TREATED WITH KID GLOVES FOR SOME REASO WELL, I DON'T! I'M ABSOLUTELY FINE!
OH, AND "PIGS IN SPACE" IS UP NEXT.
HMMM... THIS IS WEIRD. WE ORDERED A FOUR-LAYER CAKE.
AN ARTISTE DOES NOT EAT HER OWN PROPS, BUB...

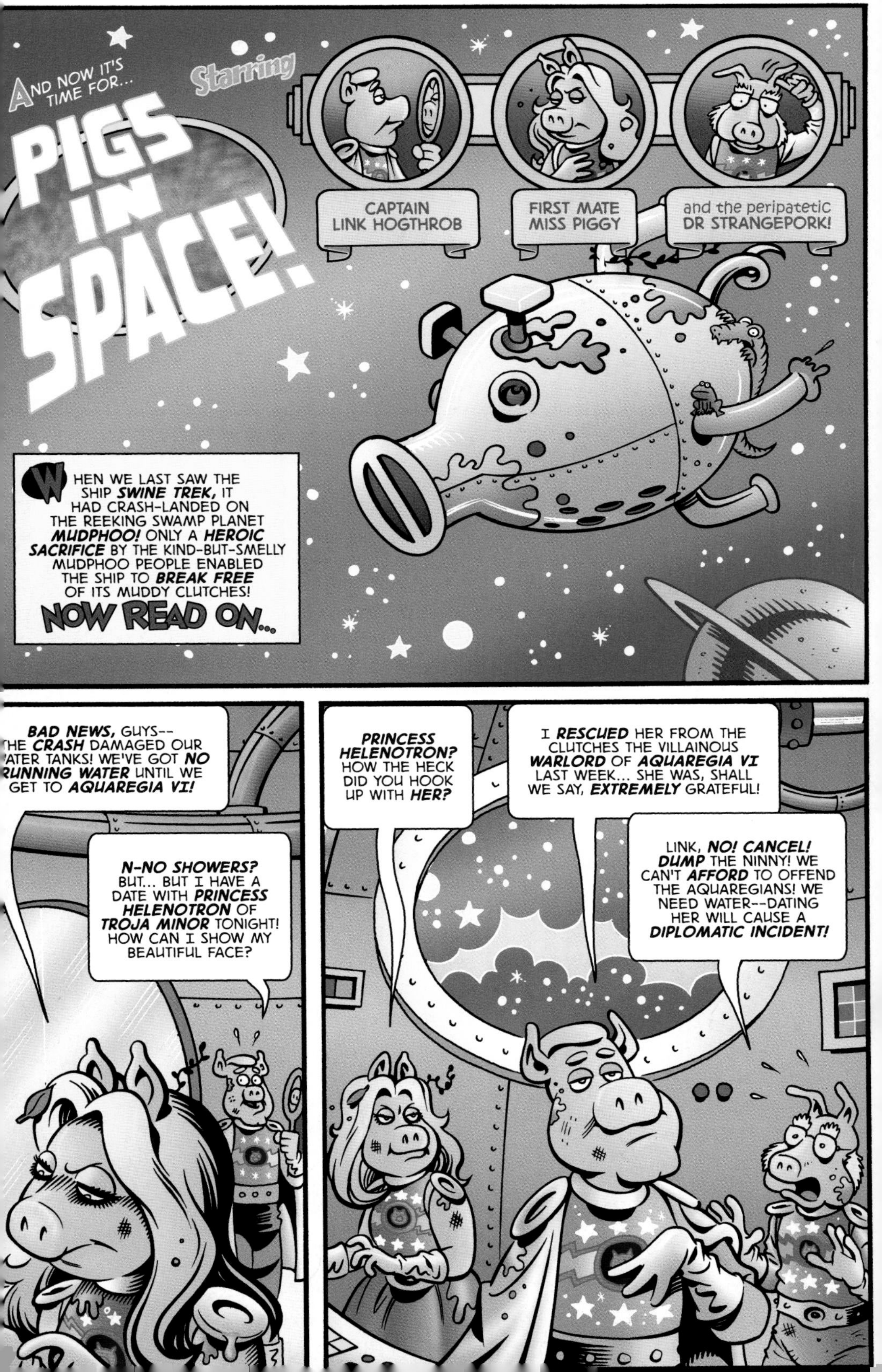
AND NOW IT'S TIME FOR...
Starring
PIGS IN SPACE!
CAPTAIN LINK HOGTHROB
FIRST MATE MISS PIGGY
and the peripatetic DR STRANGEPORK!
WHEN WE LAST SAW THE SHIP SWINE TREK, IT HAD CRASH-LANDED ON THE REEKING SWAMP PLANET MUDPHOO! ONLY A HEROIC SACRIFICE BY THE KIND-BUT-SMELLY MUDPHOO PEOPLE ENABLED THE SHIP TO BREAK FREE OF ITS MUDDY CLUTCHES!
NOW READ ON...
BAD NEWS, GUYS-- THE CRASH DAMAGED OUR ATER TANKS! WE'VE GOT NO UNNING WATER UNTIL WE GET TO AQUAREGIA VI!
N-NO SHOWERS? BUT... BUT I HAVE A DATE WITH PRINCESS HELENOTRON OF TROJA MINOR TONIGHT! HOW CAN I SHOW MY BEAUTIFUL FACE?
PRINCESS HELENOTRON? HOW THE HECK DID YOU HOOK UP WITH HER?
I RESCUED HER FROM THE CLUTCHES THE VILLAINOUS WARLORD OF AQUAREGIA VI LAST WEEK... SHE WAS, SHALL WE SAY, EXTREMELY GRATEFUL!
LINK, NO! CANCEL! DUMP THE NINNY! WE CAN'T AFFORD TO OFFEND THE AQUAREGIANS! WE NEED WATER--DATING HER WILL CAUSE A DIPLOMATIC INCIDENT!

CANCEL? ARE YOU *CRAZY?* WHY, JUST LAST MONTH SHE WAS VOTED *FACE MOST LIKELY TO START A WAR* BY *GALACTIC QUARTERLY MAGAZINE!*

THAT'S KIND OF THE *POINT!*

ANYWAY, WHAT KIND OF AN IMPRESSION WILL YOU MAKE WHEN YOU *REEK* LIKE A *BLOCKED-UP SEWER?*

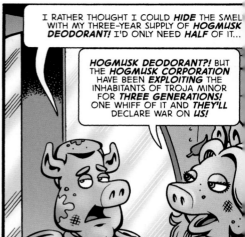

I RATHER THOUGHT I COULD *HIDE* THE SMELL WITH MY THREE-YEAR SUPPLY OF *HOGMUSK DEODORANT!* I'D ONLY NEED *HALF* OF IT...

HOGMUSK DEODORANT?! BUT THE *HOGMUSK CORPORATION* HAVE BEEN *EXPLOITING* THE INHABITANTS OF TROJA MINOR FOR *THREE GENERATIONS!* ONE WHIFF OF IT AND *THEY'LL* DECLARE WAR ON *US!*

B-BUT PRINCESS HELENOTRON HAS A *MARBLE HOT TUB...*

MARBLE?! NOT *VENUSIAN MARBLE,* I HOPE! THEY MAKE THAT STUFF FROM *PUPPY DOG TAILS!*

HE'S *RIGHT,* CAPTAIN! YOU COULD HAVE THE *DOGSTAR MILITIA* COME DOWN ON *BOTH* PLANETS LIKE A *TON OF SAINT BERNARDS!*

≷SIGH≶ I GIVE UP. IS THERE ANYTHING I CAN DO THAT *WON'T* CAUSE AN INTERPLANETARY INCIDENT?

HMMM... DO YOU THINK I'M GETTING BAGS UNDER MY EYES?

OH, WELL... THERE ARE *WORSE* WAYS TO SPEND AN EVENING.

FINGERS CROSSED, LINK... FINGERS CROSSED.

WILL CAPTAIN LIN HOGTHRO AND PRINCE HELENOTRON EVE GET NEAR THAT MARBLE HOT TUB

WILL DOCTOR STRANGEPO CANCEL H SUBSCRIPTION *GALACTIC QUARTE.*

WILL FIRST MATE PIGGY EVE BE CLEAN ENOUGH TO SIT IN CAKE AGAIN? HOLD THIS EPISODE UP TO MIRROR SO YOU WON'T NEED TO READ THE NEXT EPISODE OF...

PIGS IN SPAAACE

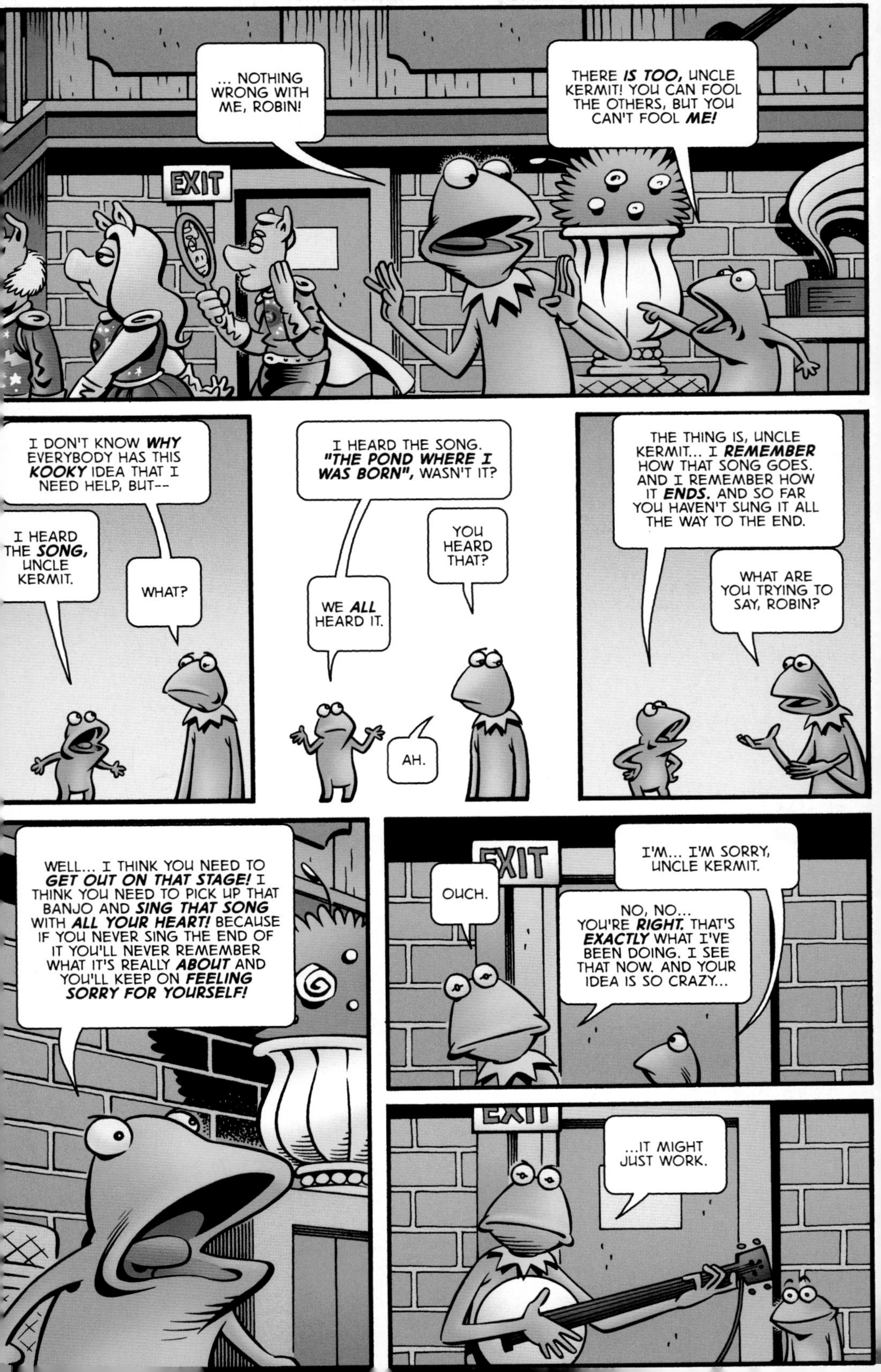
... NOTHING WRONG WITH ME, ROBIN!
THERE IS TOO, UNCLE KERMIT! YOU CAN FOOL THE OTHERS, BUT YOU CAN'T FOOL ME!
EXIT
I DON'T KNOW WHY EVERYBODY HAS THIS KOOKY IDEA THAT I NEED HELP, BUT--
I HEARD THE SONG, UNCLE KERMIT.
WHAT?
I HEARD THE SONG. "THE POND WHERE I WAS BORN", WASN'T IT?
YOU HEARD THAT?
WE ALL HEARD IT.
AH.
THE THING IS, UNCLE KERMIT... I REMEMBER HOW THAT SONG GOES. AND I REMEMBER HOW IT ENDS. AND SO FAR YOU HAVEN'T SUNG IT ALL THE WAY TO THE END.
WHAT ARE YOU TRYING TO SAY, ROBIN?
WELL... I THINK YOU NEED TO GET OUT ON THAT STAGE! I THINK YOU NEED TO PICK UP THAT BANJO AND SING THAT SONG WITH ALL YOUR HEART! BECAUSE IF YOU NEVER SING THE END OF IT YOU'LL NEVER REMEMBER WHAT IT'S REALLY ABOUT AND YOU'LL KEEP ON FEELING SORRY FOR YOURSELF!
EXIT
OUCH.
I'M... I'M SORRY, UNCLE KERMIT.
NO, NO... YOU'RE RIGHT. THAT'S EXACTLY WHAT I'VE BEEN DOING. I SEE THAT NOW. AND YOUR IDEA IS SO CRAZY...
...IT MIGHT JUST WORK.

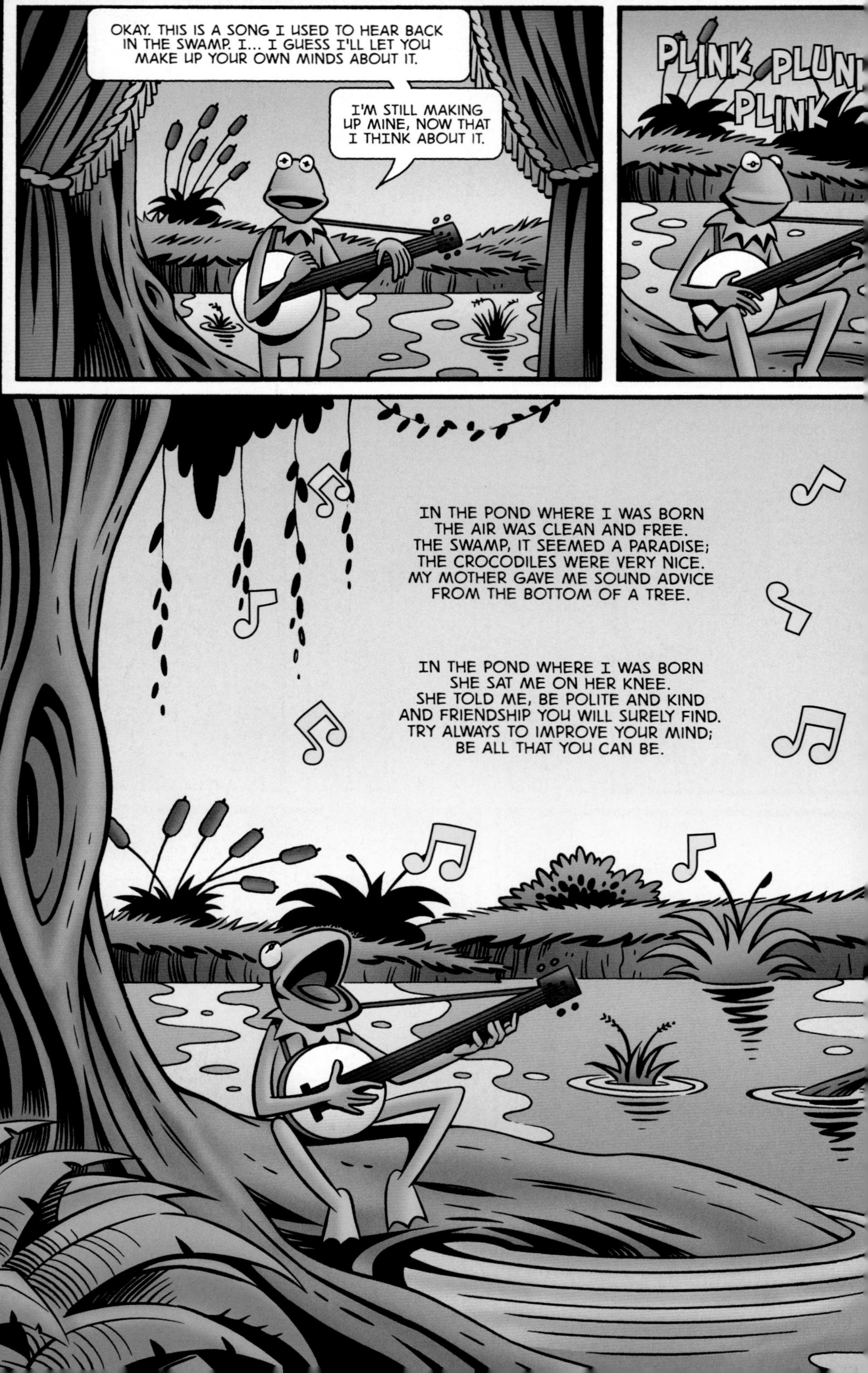
OKAY. THIS IS A SONG I USED TO HEAR BACK IN THE SWAMP. I... I GUESS I'LL LET YOU MAKE UP YOUR OWN MINDS ABOUT IT.
I'M STILL MAKING UP MINE, NOW THAT I THINK ABOUT IT.
PLINK PLUN
PLINK
IN THE POND WHERE I WAS BORN
THE AIR WAS CLEAN AND FREE.
THE SWAMP, IT SEEMED A PARADISE;
THE CROCODILES WERE VERY NICE.
MY MOTHER GAVE ME SOUND ADVICE
FROM THE BOTTOM OF A TREE.
IN THE POND WHERE I WAS BORN
SHE SAT ME ON HER KNEE.
SHE TOLD ME, BE POLITE AND KIND
AND FRIENDSHIP YOU WILL SURELY FIND.
TRY ALWAYS TO IMPROVE YOUR MIND;
BE ALL THAT YOU CAN BE.

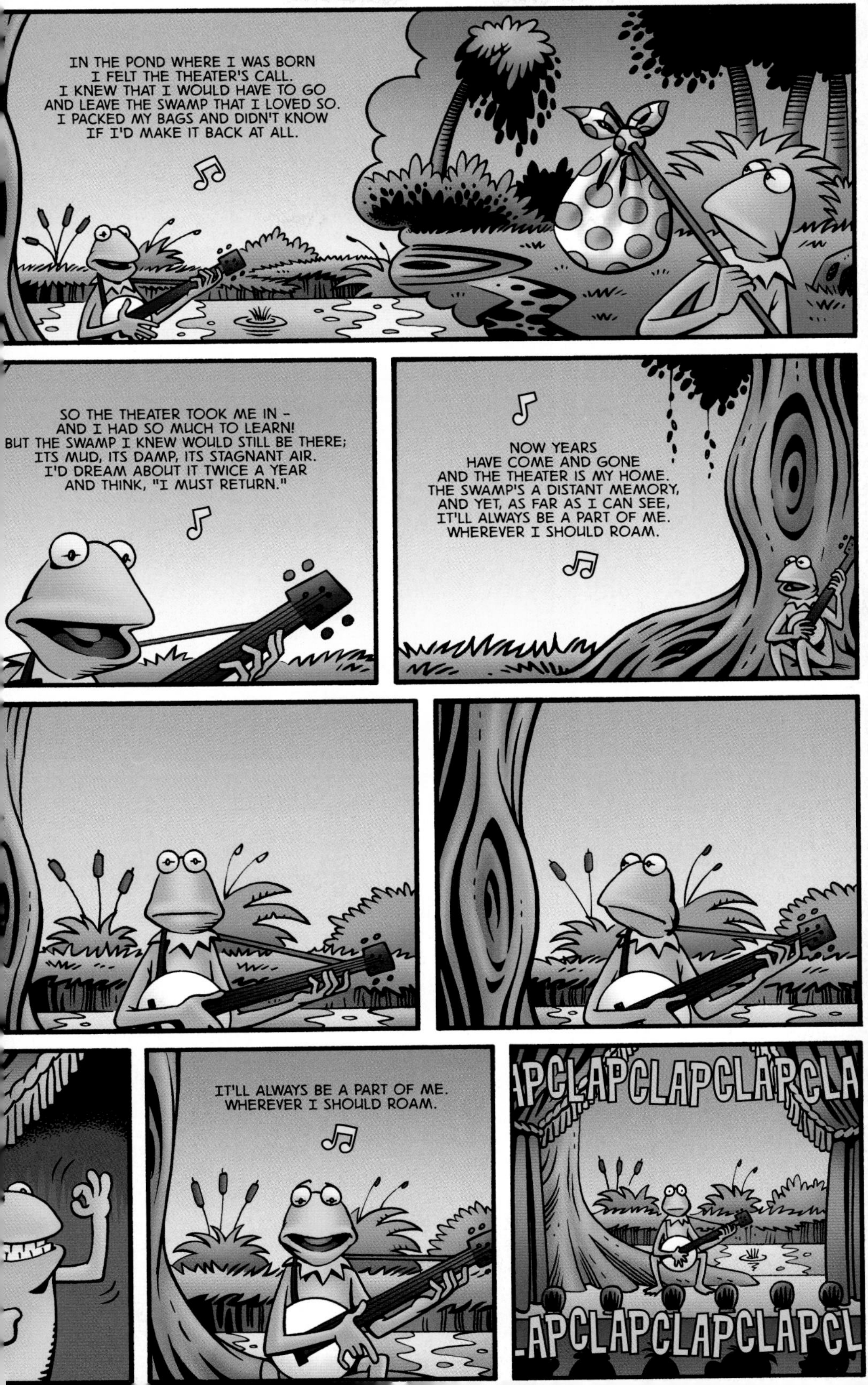
IN THE POND WHERE I WAS BORN
I FELT THE THEATER'S CALL.
I KNEW THAT I WOULD HAVE TO GO
AND LEAVE THE SWAMP THAT I LOVED SO.
I PACKED MY BAGS AND DIDN'T KNOW
IF I'D MAKE IT BACK AT ALL.
SO THE THEATER TOOK ME IN -
AND I HAD SO MUCH TO LEARN!
BUT THE SWAMP I KNEW WOULD STILL BE THERE;
ITS MUD, ITS DAMP, ITS STAGNANT AIR.
I'D DREAM ABOUT IT TWICE A YEAR
AND THINK, "I MUST RETURN."
NOW YEARS
HAVE COME AND GONE
AND THE THEATER IS MY HOME.
THE SWAMP'S A DISTANT MEMORY,
AND YET, AS FAR AS I CAN SEE,
IT'LL ALWAYS BE A PART OF ME.
WHEREVER I SHOULD ROAM.
IT'LL ALWAYS BE A PART OF ME.
WHEREVER I SHOULD ROAM.
APCLAPCLAPCLAPCLA
APCLAPCLAPCLAPCL

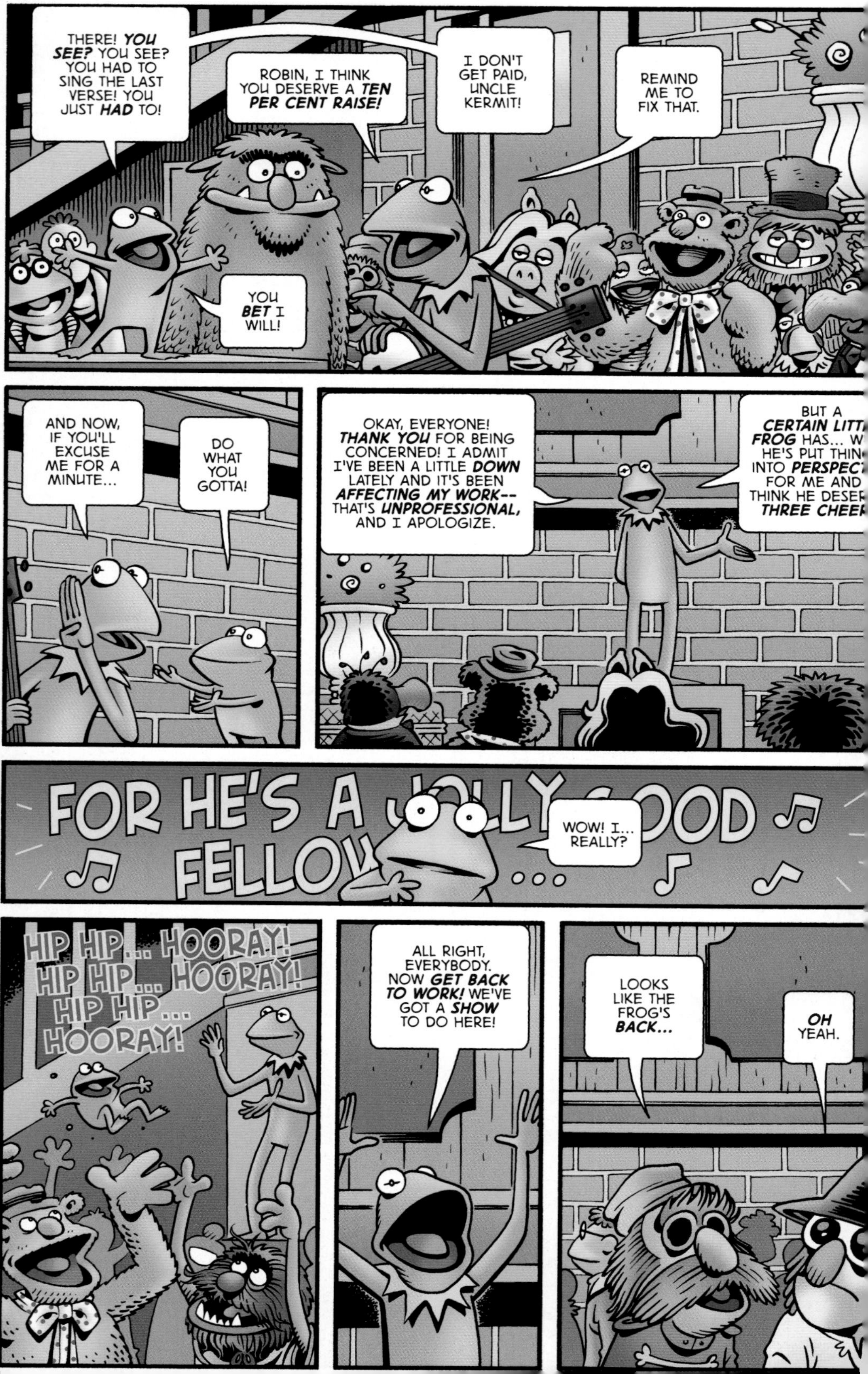
THERE! YOU SEE? YOU SEE? YOU HAD TO SING THE LAST VERSE! YOU JUST HAD TO!
ROBIN, I THINK YOU DESERVE A TEN PER CENT RAISE!
I DON'T GET PAID, UNCLE KERMIT!
REMIND ME TO FIX THAT.
YOU BET I WILL!
AND NOW, IF YOU'LL EXCUSE ME FOR A MINUTE...
DO WHAT YOU GOTTA!
OKAY, EVERYONE! THANK YOU FOR BEING CONCERNED! I ADMIT I'VE BEEN A LITTLE DOWN LATELY AND IT'S BEEN AFFECTING MY WORK-- THAT'S UNPROFESSIONAL, AND I APOLOGIZE.
BUT A CERTAIN LITT FROG HAS... W HE'S PUT THIN INTO PERSPEC FOR ME AND THINK HE DESER THREE CHEER
FOR HE'S A JOLLY GOOD FELLOW...
WOW! I... REALLY?
HIP HIP... HOORAY! HIP HIP... HOORAY! HIP HIP... HOORAY!
ALL RIGHT, EVERYBODY. NOW GET BACK TO WORK! WE'VE GOT A SHOW TO DO HERE!
LOOKS LIKE THE FROG'S BACK...
OH YEAH.

LATER...

PLINKA PLUNKA
PLINK A
PLINK

PLINKA PLUNKA
PLINKA PLINK
PLONK

HEY, UNCLE KERMIT. MIND IF I JOIN YOU?

MMM? OH, HI, ROBIN. SURE, BE MY GUEST.

I'M GLAD YOU'RE FEELING BETTER. BUT THERE'S STILL ONE THING I WANNA KNOW.

SHOOT.

WELL... WHAT WAS IN THAT *LETTER* THAT MADE YOU SO GLUM IN THE *FIRST* PLACE?

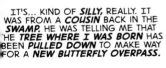

IT'S... KIND OF *SILLY*, REALLY. IT WAS FROM A *COUSIN* BACK IN THE *SWAMP*. HE WAS TELLING ME THAT THE *TREE WHERE I WAS BORN* HAS BEEN *PULLED DOWN* TO MAKE WAY FOR A *NEW BUTTERFLY OVERPASS*.

AND IT HIT ME THAT I CAN NEVER GO *BACK*.

SURE YOU CAN. THE *SWAMP* IS STILL THERE. ALL THE PEOPLE YOU *KNOW* ARE STILL THERE.

OH, I KNOW, I KNOW. THAT'S NOT QUITE WHAT I MEAN.

IT'S MORE ABOUT A *STATE OF MIND*. SOMEWHERE AT THE BACK OF MY HEAD I KIND OF THOUGHT THAT EVERYTHING WOULD STILL BE THE *SAME* IF I EVER WENT *HOME*.

NOW I KNOW IT *WON'T*. AND THAT'S A SHAME. I FELT LIKE I'D LOST SOMETHING IMPORTANT.

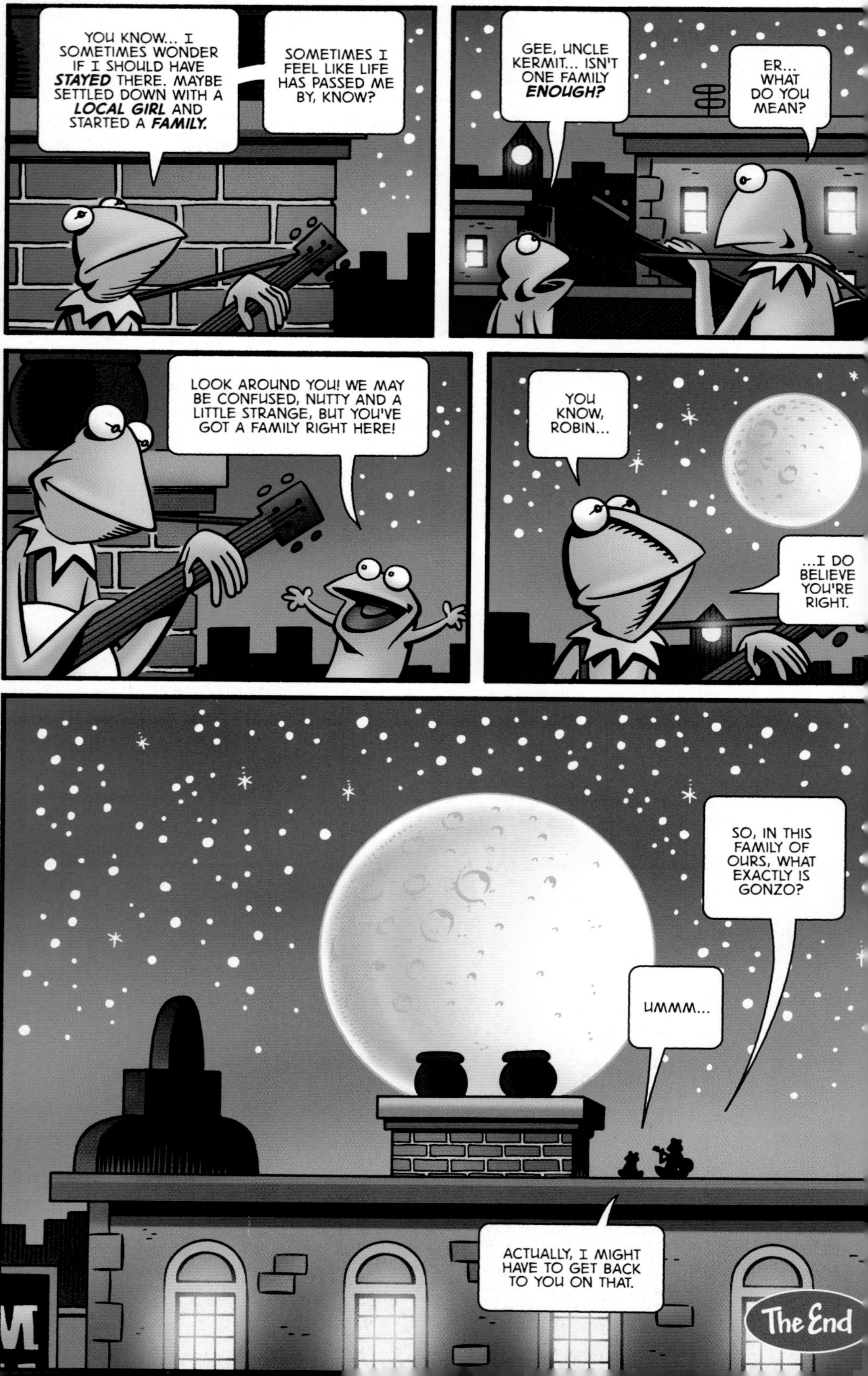
YOU KNOW... I SOMETIMES WONDER IF I SHOULD HAVE **STAYED** THERE. MAYBE SETTLED DOWN WITH A **LOCAL GIRL** AND STARTED A **FAMILY.**
SOMETIMES I FEEL LIKE LIFE HAS PASSED ME BY, KNOW?
GEE, UNCLE KERMIT... ISN'T ONE FAMILY **ENOUGH?**
ER... WHAT DO YOU MEAN?
LOOK AROUND YOU! WE MAY BE CONFUSED, NUTTY AND A LITTLE STRANGE, BUT YOU'VE GOT A FAMILY RIGHT HERE!
YOU KNOW, ROBIN...
...I DO BELIEVE YOU'RE RIGHT.
SO, IN THIS FAMILY OF OURS, WHAT EXACTLY IS GONZO?
UMMM...
ACTUALLY, I MIGHT HAVE TO GET BACK TO YOU ON THAT.
The End

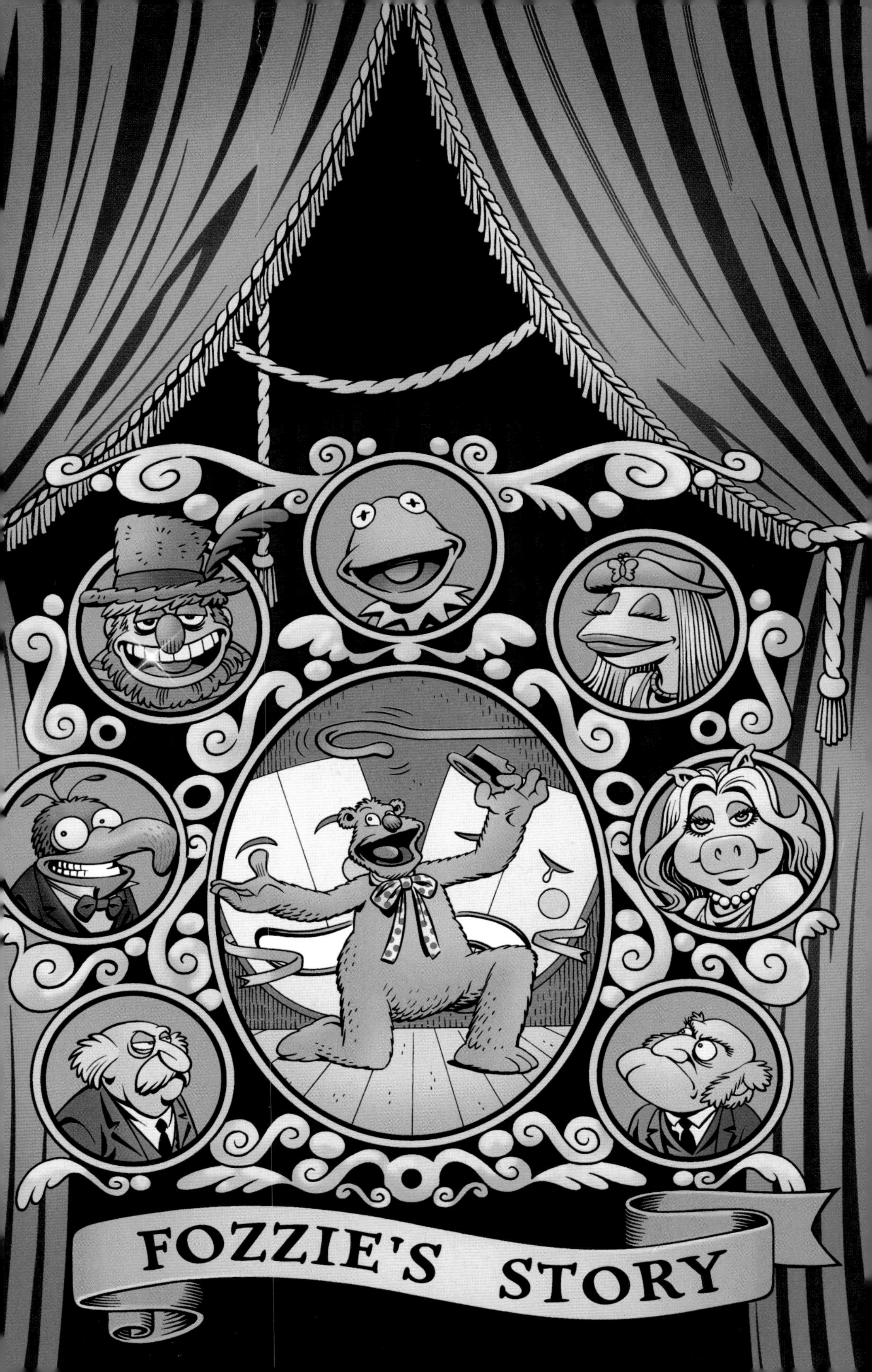
FOZZIE'S STORY

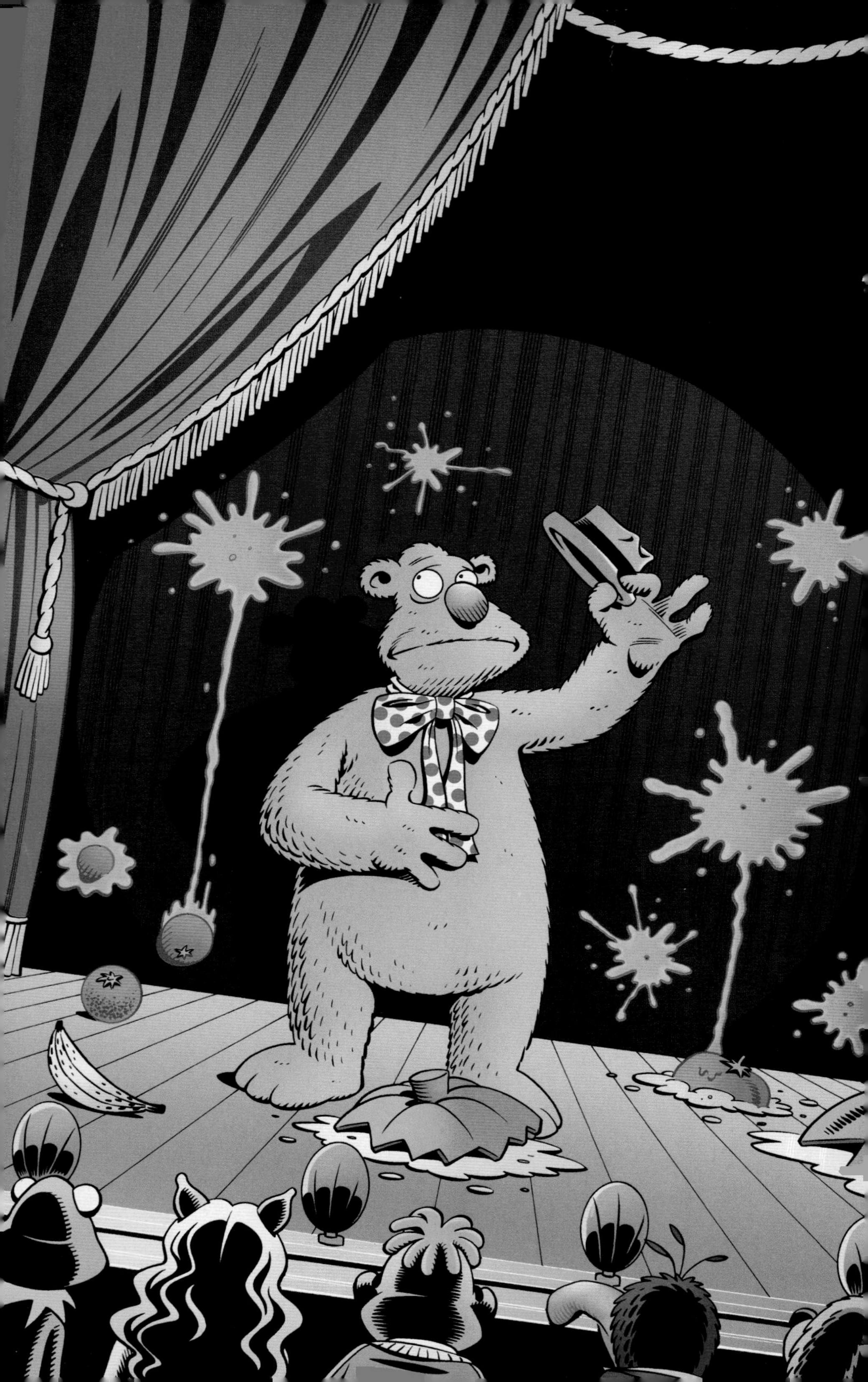

YOU KNOW, I'VE ACTUALLY BEEN LOOKING **FORWARD** TO THIS SHOW!
HEH! WELL, I GUESS OLD AGE CATCHES UP WITH THE **BEST** OF US!
YUP...IT'S A LITTLE ODD. I KEEP THINKING ABOUT THE **SONGS...**THE **SPECTACLE...**THE **GLAMOUR...**
THEY CAN BE PRETTY SPIFFY WHEN THEY WANT TO BE!
...AND THEN I REMEMBER...
OH, NO, WAIT, DON'T TELL ME...
...THE JOKES.
OOOOHHH.
THIS SHOW IS GOING TO BE ABSOLUTELY **TERRIBLE,** ISN'T IT?
YOU HIT THE NAIL RIGHT INTO THE LID.

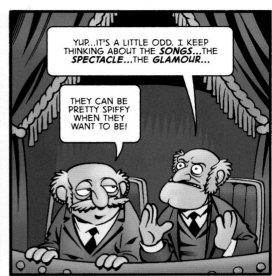

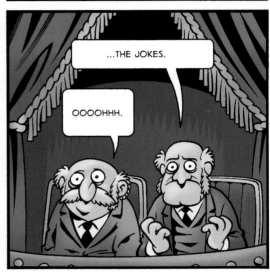

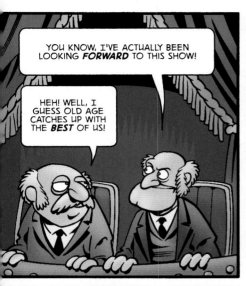

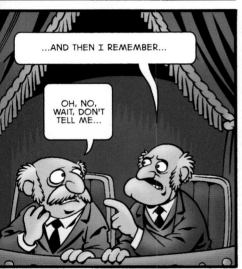

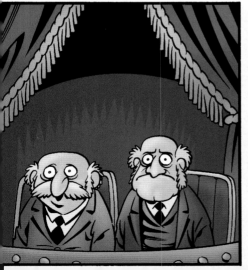

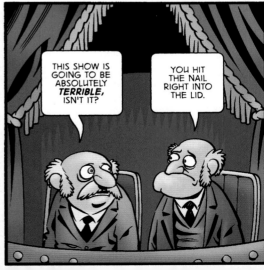

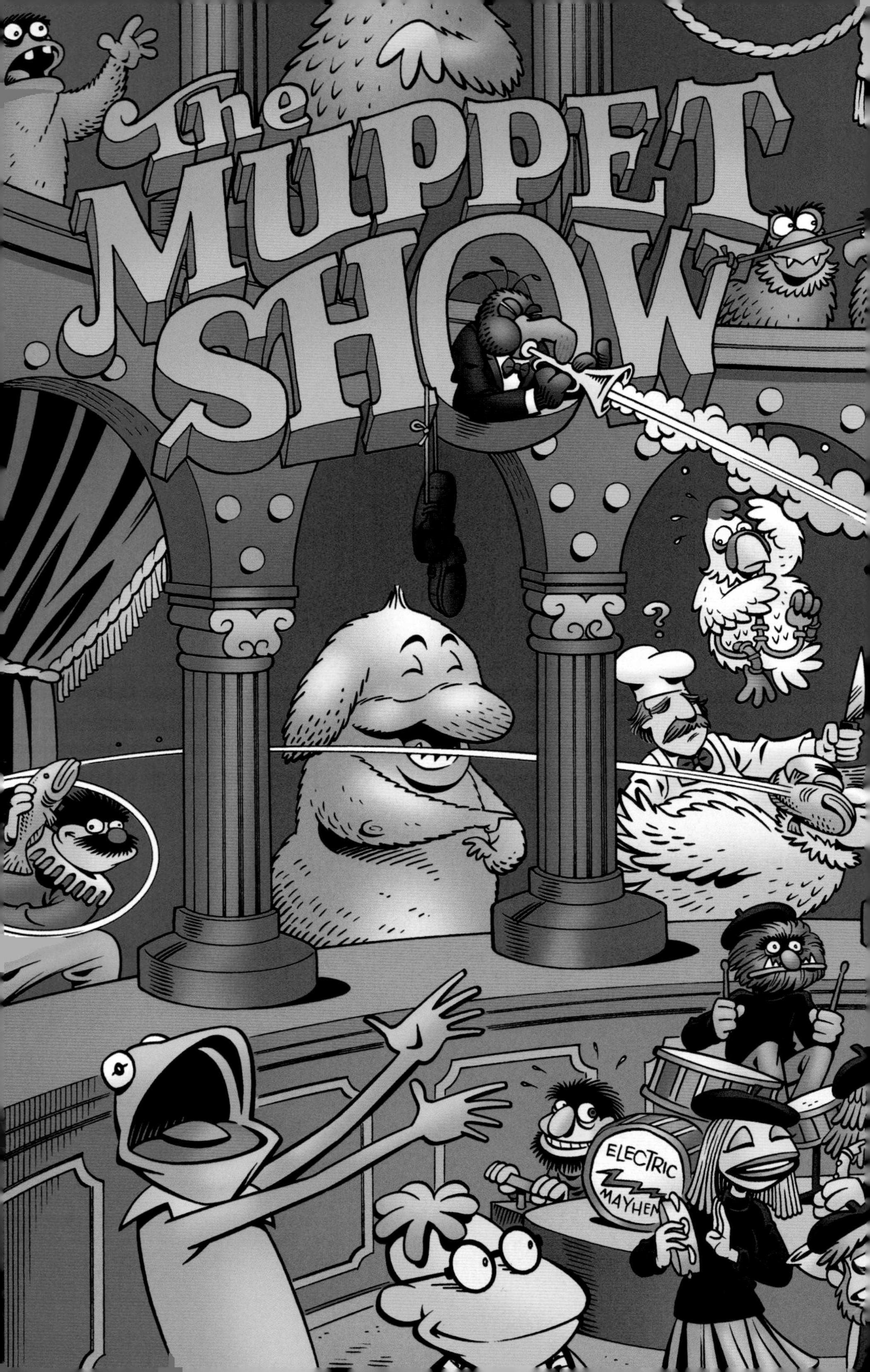
The
MUPPET
SHOW
?
ELECTRIC
MAYHEM

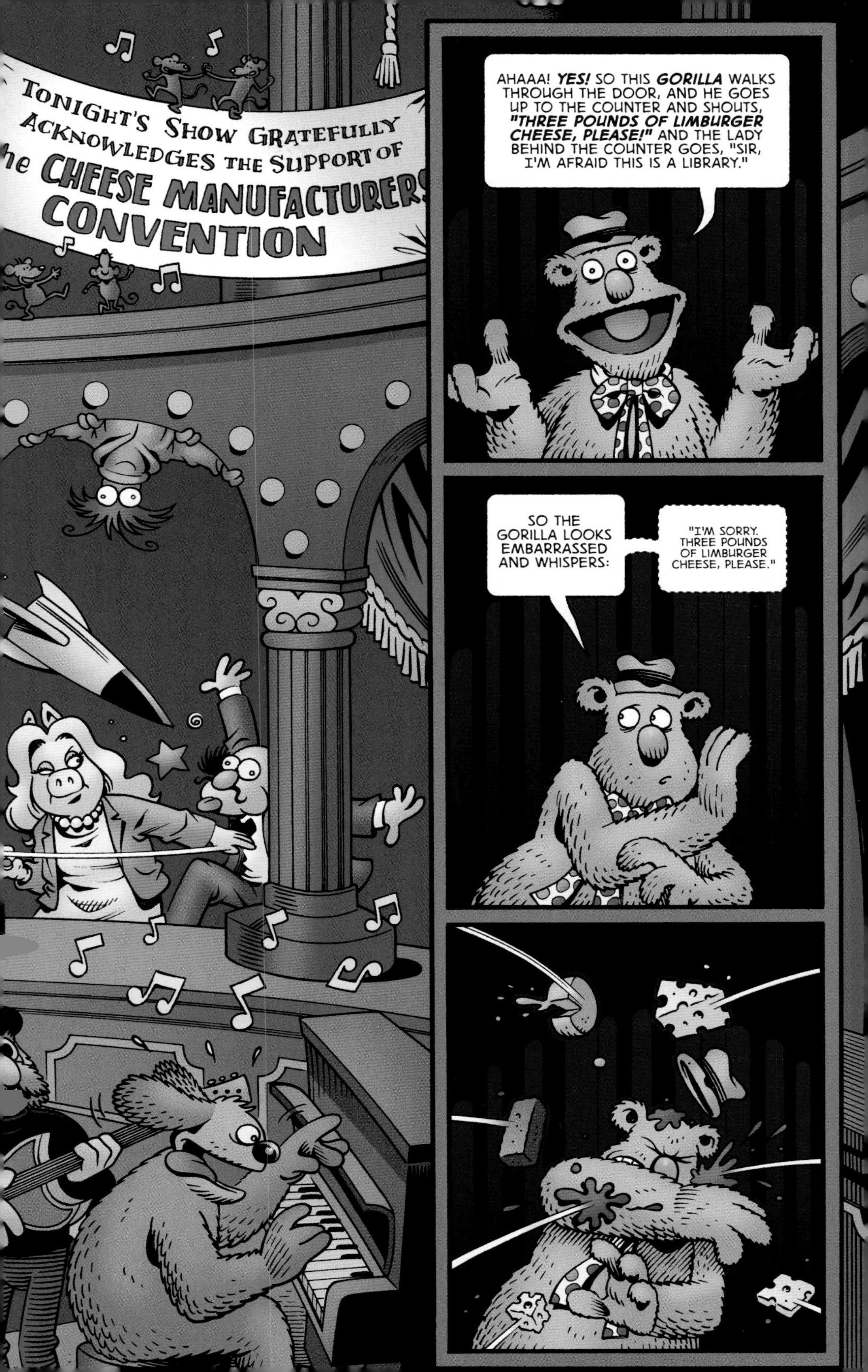

TONIGHT'S SHOW GRATEFULLY ACKNOWLEDGES THE SUPPORT OF the CHEESE MANUFACTURERS CONVENTION
AHAAA! YES! SO THIS GORILLA WALKS THROUGH THE DOOR, AND HE GOES UP TO THE COUNTER AND SHOUTS, "THREE POUNDS OF LIMBURGER CHEESE, PLEASE!" AND THE LADY BEHIND THE COUNTER GOES, "SIR, I'M AFRAID THIS IS A LIBRARY."
SO THE GORILLA LOOKS EMBARRASSED AND WHISPERS:
"I'M SORRY. THREE POUNDS OF LIMBURGER CHEESE, PLEASE."

NICE WORK, GUYS! ALMOST PROFESSIONAL STANDARD THIS TIME! LOSE THE CASUAL VIOLENCE AND WE MIGHT YET MAKE IT.

OH, KERMIT. OH MY OH MY OH MY.

THEY HATED ME! HATED ME! TELL ME, KERMIT-- AS A FRIEND--DO YOU THINK I'VE LOST MY TOUCH?

HONESTLY?

I WOULDN'T WORRY IF I WERE YOU. I JUST THINK YOU WERE PUSHING IT WITH THE CHEESE GAGS. WE'VE GOT A CROWD FROM THE CHEESE MANUFACTURERS' CONVENTION OUT THERE-- THEY'RE A SENSITIVE BUNCH.

OH, KERMIT! I WISH IT WERE THAT SIMPLE!

NO... I'M CONVINCED THAT MY ACT NEEDS TO BE REINVENTED FROM FIRST PRINCIPLES! IF MY OLD SET ISN'T GOOD ENOUGH FOR THEM, I'LL JUST HAVE TO FIND ANOTHER ONE!

WELL, I'LL LEAVE IT TO YOU, FOZZIE. I'M SURE YOU KNOW WHAT YOU'RE DOING.

LATER...

AAGHH! I WISH I KNEW WHAT I WAS DOING!

FOZZIE BEAR

≥SIGH≤ MAYBE THE OL' LIBRARY HAS A CLUE OR TWO. I NEED INSPIRATION!

OHO! AHA! YES! YES! MAYBE I DON'T KNOW WHAT I'M DOING--BUT NOBODY COULD EVER SAY THAT WILLIAM SHAKESPEARE WASN'T FUNNY!

WHERE'S MY NOTEBOOK? I'VE GOT A SET TO WRITE!

NEXT:

IN MY MERR

OLDSMOB

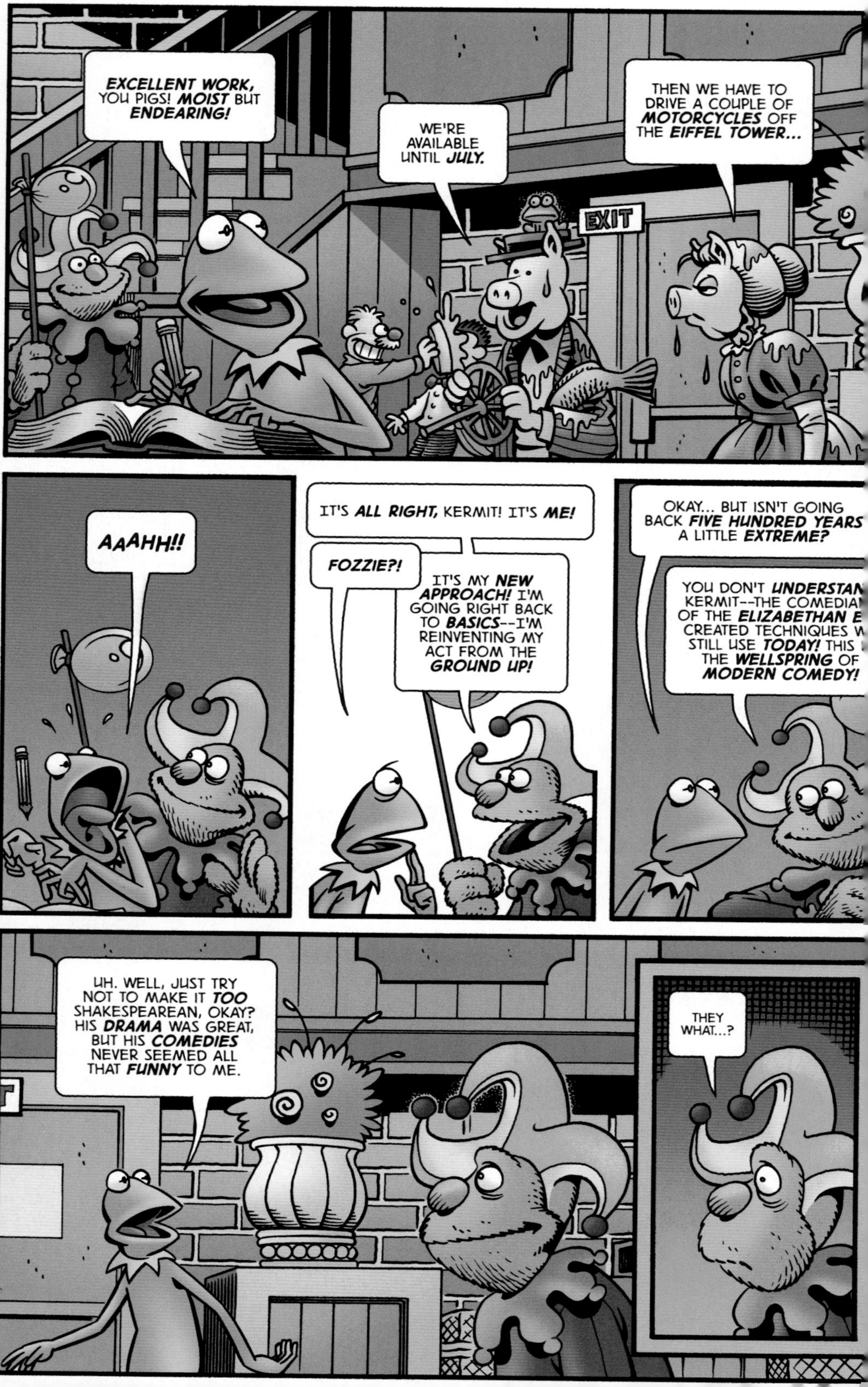
EXCELLENT WORK, YOU PIGS! MOIST BUT ENDEARING!
WE'RE AVAILABLE UNTIL JULY.
THEN WE HAVE TO DRIVE A COUPLE OF MOTORCYCLES OFF THE EIFFEL TOWER...
EXIT
AAAHH!!
IT'S ALL RIGHT, KERMIT! IT'S ME!
FOZZIE?!
IT'S MY NEW APPROACH! I'M GOING RIGHT BACK TO BASICS--I'M REINVENTING MY ACT FROM THE GROUND UP!
OKAY... BUT ISN'T GOING BACK FIVE HUNDRED YEARS A LITTLE EXTREME?
YOU DON'T UNDERSTAN KERMIT--THE COMEDIA OF THE ELIZABETHAN E CREATED TECHNIQUES W STILL USE TODAY! THIS THE WELLSPRING OF MODERN COMEDY!
UH. WELL, JUST TRY NOT TO MAKE IT TOO SHAKESPEAREAN, OKAY? HIS DRAMA WAS GREAT, BUT HIS COMEDIES NEVER SEEMED ALL THAT FUNNY TO ME.
THEY WHAT...?

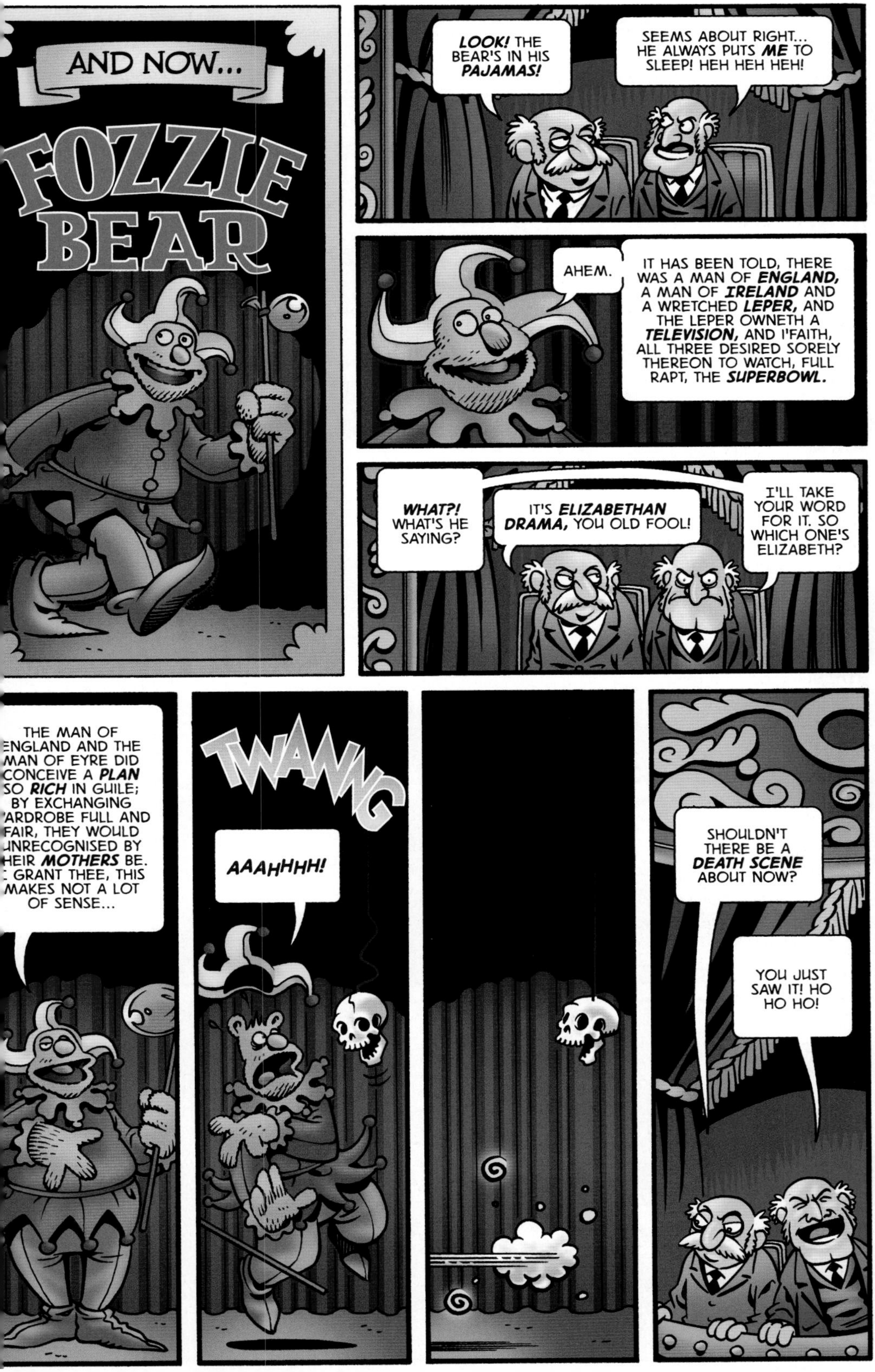

AND NOW...
FOZZIE BEAR
LOOK! THE BEAR'S IN HIS PAJAMAS!
SEEMS ABOUT RIGHT... HE ALWAYS PUTS ME TO SLEEP! HEH HEH HEH!
AHEM.
IT HAS BEEN TOLD, THERE WAS A MAN OF ENGLAND, A MAN OF IRELAND AND A WRETCHED LEPER, AND THE LEPER OWNETH A TELEVISION, AND I'FAITH, ALL THREE DESIRED SORELY THEREON TO WATCH, FULL RAPT, THE SUPERBOWL.
WHAT?! WHAT'S HE SAYING?
IT'S ELIZABETHAN DRAMA, YOU OLD FOOL!
I'LL TAKE YOUR WORD FOR IT. SO WHICH ONE'S ELIZABETH?
THE MAN OF ENGLAND AND THE MAN OF EYRE DID CONCEIVE A PLAN SO RICH IN GUILE; BY EXCHANGING ARDROBE FULL AND FAIR, THEY WOULD UNRECOGNISED BY HEIR MOTHERS BE. GRANT THEE, THIS MAKES NOT A LOT OF SENSE...
TWANNG
AAAHHHH!
SHOULDN'T THERE BE A DEATH SCENE ABOUT NOW?
YOU JUST SAW IT! HO HO HO!

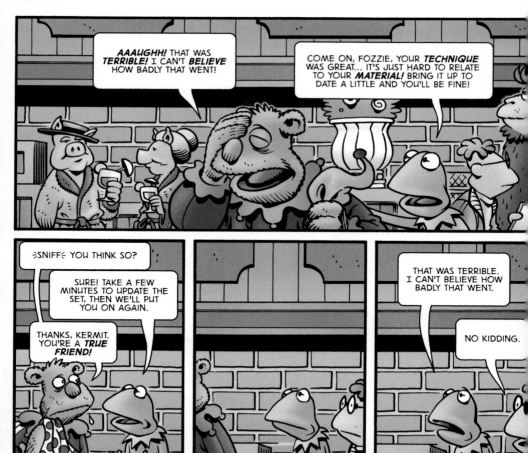

AAAUGHH! THAT WAS **TERRIBLE!** I CAN'T **BELIEVE** HOW BADLY THAT WENT!

COME ON, FOZZIE, YOUR **TECHNIQUE** WAS GREAT... IT'S JUST HARD TO RELATE TO YOUR **MATERIAL!** BRING IT UP TO DATE A LITTLE AND YOU'LL BE FINE!

≥SNIFF≤ YOU THINK SO?

SURE! TAKE A FEW MINUTES TO UPDATE THE SET, THEN WE'LL PUT YOU ON AGAIN.

THANKS, KERMIT. YOU'RE A **TRUE FRIEND!**

THAT WAS TERRIBLE. I CAN'T BELIEVE HOW BADLY THAT WENT.

NO KIDDING.

OKAY, OKAY... MAYBE KERMIT'S RIGHT. LET'S RE-THINK THIS A LITTLE...

AHUM... AHUM... YUP...

DAN LENO
HOW I EARN FOUR SHILL A YEAR BY MOCKING THE WORKING CLASSES

A-**HA!**

NEXT:

MUPPET LABS

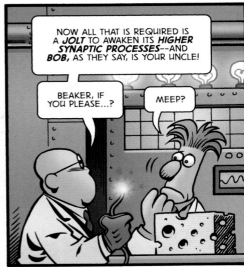

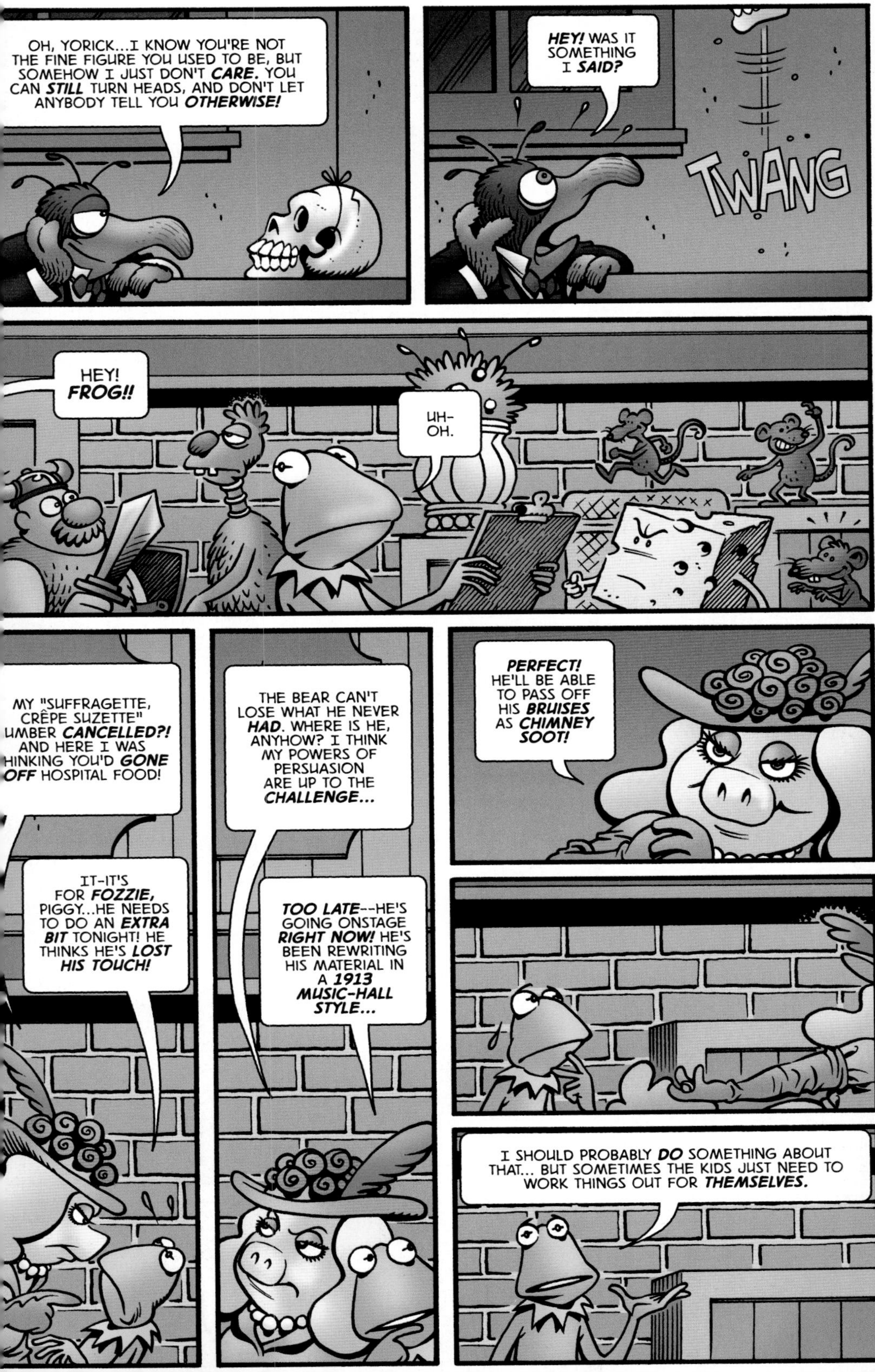
OH, YORICK...I KNOW YOU'RE NOT THE FINE FIGURE YOU USED TO BE, BUT SOMEHOW I JUST DON'T CARE. YOU CAN STILL TURN HEADS, AND DON'T LET ANYBODY TELL YOU OTHERWISE!
HEY! WAS IT SOMETHING I SAID?
TWANG
HEY! FROG!!
UH-OH.
MY "SUFFRAGETTE, CRÊPE SUZETTE" UMBER CANCELLED?! AND HERE I WAS HINKING YOU'D GONE OFF HOSPITAL FOOD!
IT-IT'S FOR FOZZIE, PIGGY...HE NEEDS TO DO AN EXTRA BIT TONIGHT! HE THINKS HE'S LOST HIS TOUCH!
THE BEAR CAN'T LOSE WHAT HE NEVER HAD. WHERE IS HE, ANYHOW? I THINK MY POWERS OF PERSUASION ARE UP TO THE CHALLENGE...
TOO LATE--HE'S GOING ONSTAGE RIGHT NOW! HE'S BEEN REWRITING HIS MATERIAL IN A 1913 MUSIC-HALL STYLE...
PERFECT! HE'LL BE ABLE TO PASS OFF HIS BRUISES AS CHIMNEY SOOT!
I SHOULD PROBABLY DO SOMETHING ABOUT THAT... BUT SOMETIMES THE KIDS JUST NEED TO WORK THINGS OUT FOR THEMSELVES.

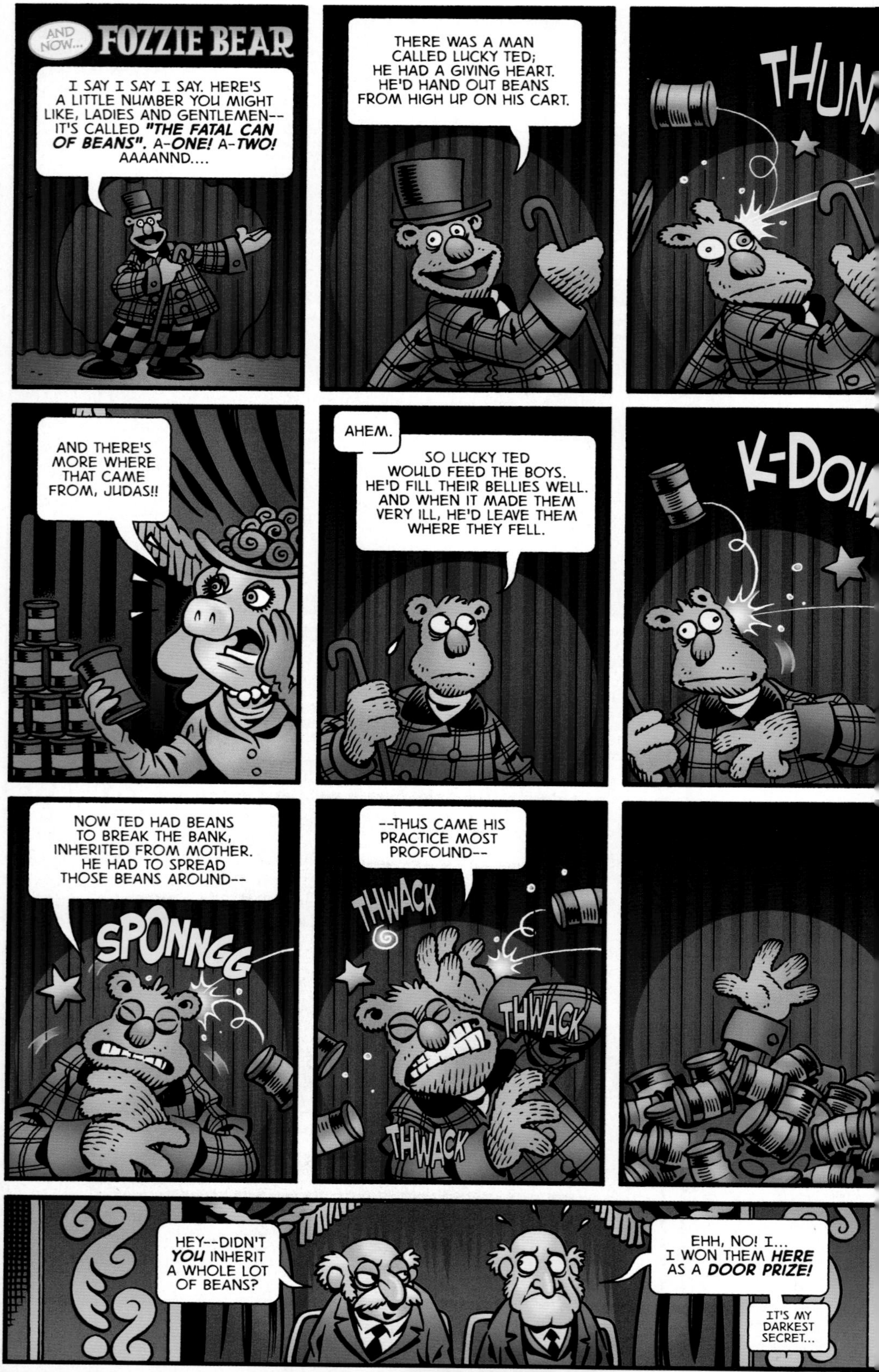

AND NOW...
FOZZIE BEAR
I SAY I SAY I SAY. HERE'S A LITTLE NUMBER YOU MIGHT LIKE, LADIES AND GENTLEMEN-- IT'S CALLED "THE FATAL CAN OF BEANS". A-ONE! A-TWO! AAAAANND....
THERE WAS A MAN CALLED LUCKY TED; HE HAD A GIVING HEART. HE'D HAND OUT BEANS FROM HIGH UP ON HIS CART.
THUN
AND THERE'S MORE WHERE THAT CAME FROM, JUDAS!!
AHEM.
SO LUCKY TED WOULD FEED THE BOYS. HE'D FILL THEIR BELLIES WELL. AND WHEN IT MADE THEM VERY ILL, HE'D LEAVE THEM WHERE THEY FELL.
K-DOIN
NOW TED HAD BEANS TO BREAK THE BANK, INHERITED FROM MOTHER. HE HAD TO SPREAD THOSE BEANS AROUND--
SPONNGG
--THUS CAME HIS PRACTICE MOST PROFOUND--
THWACK
THWACK
THWACK
HEY--DIDN'T YOU INHERIT A WHOLE LOT OF BEANS?
EHH, NO! I... I WON THEM HERE AS A DOOR PRIZE!
IT'S MY DARKEST SECRET...

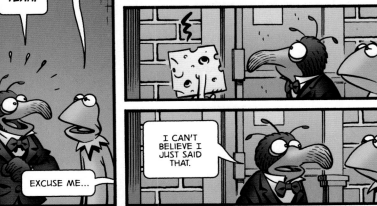

The UBIQUITOUS QUIL

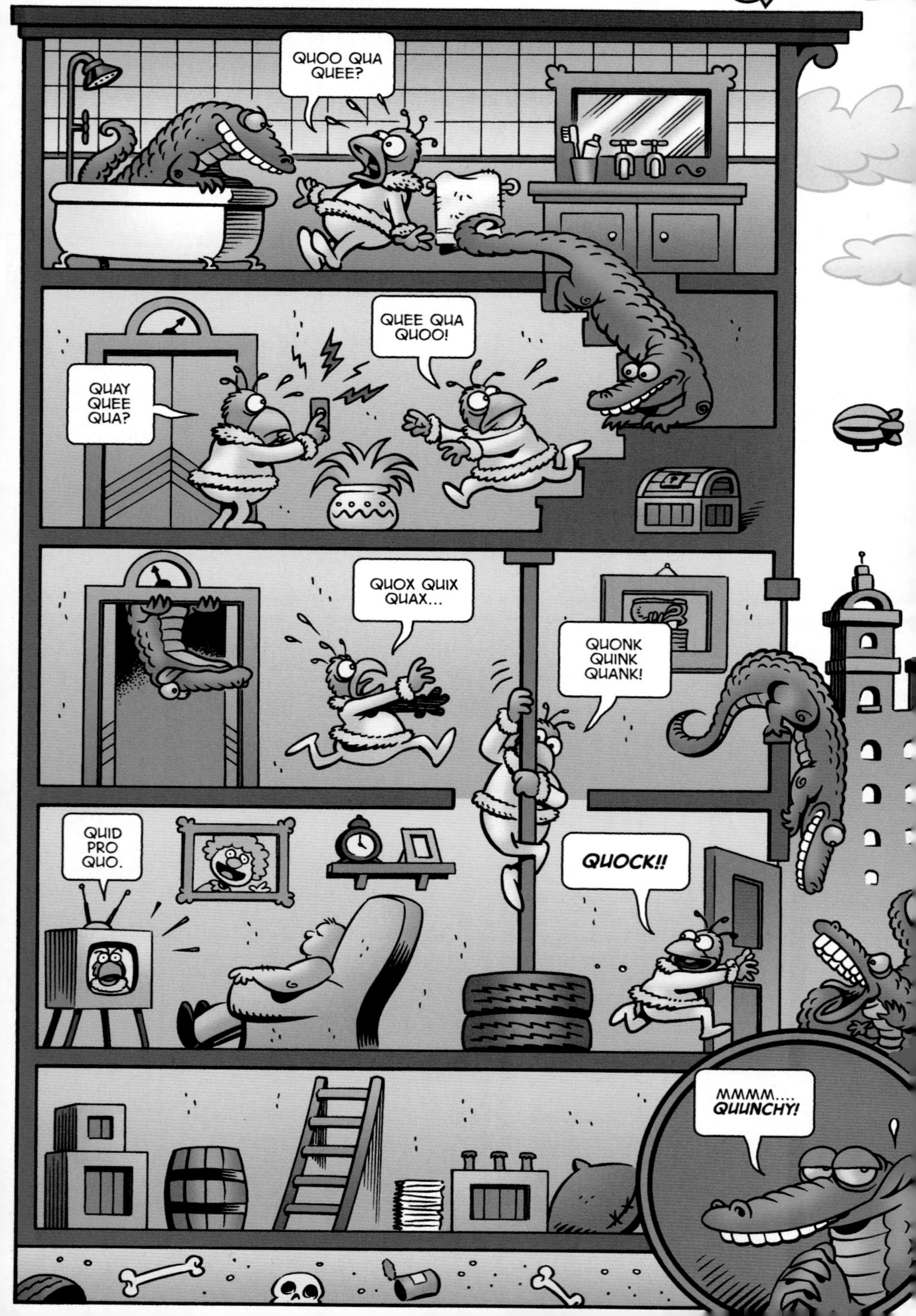

QUOO QUA QUEE?
QUAY QUEE QUA?
QUEE QUA QUOO!
QUOX QUIX QUAX...
QUONK QUINK QUANK!
QUID PRO QUO.
QUOCK!!
MMMM.... QUUNCHY!

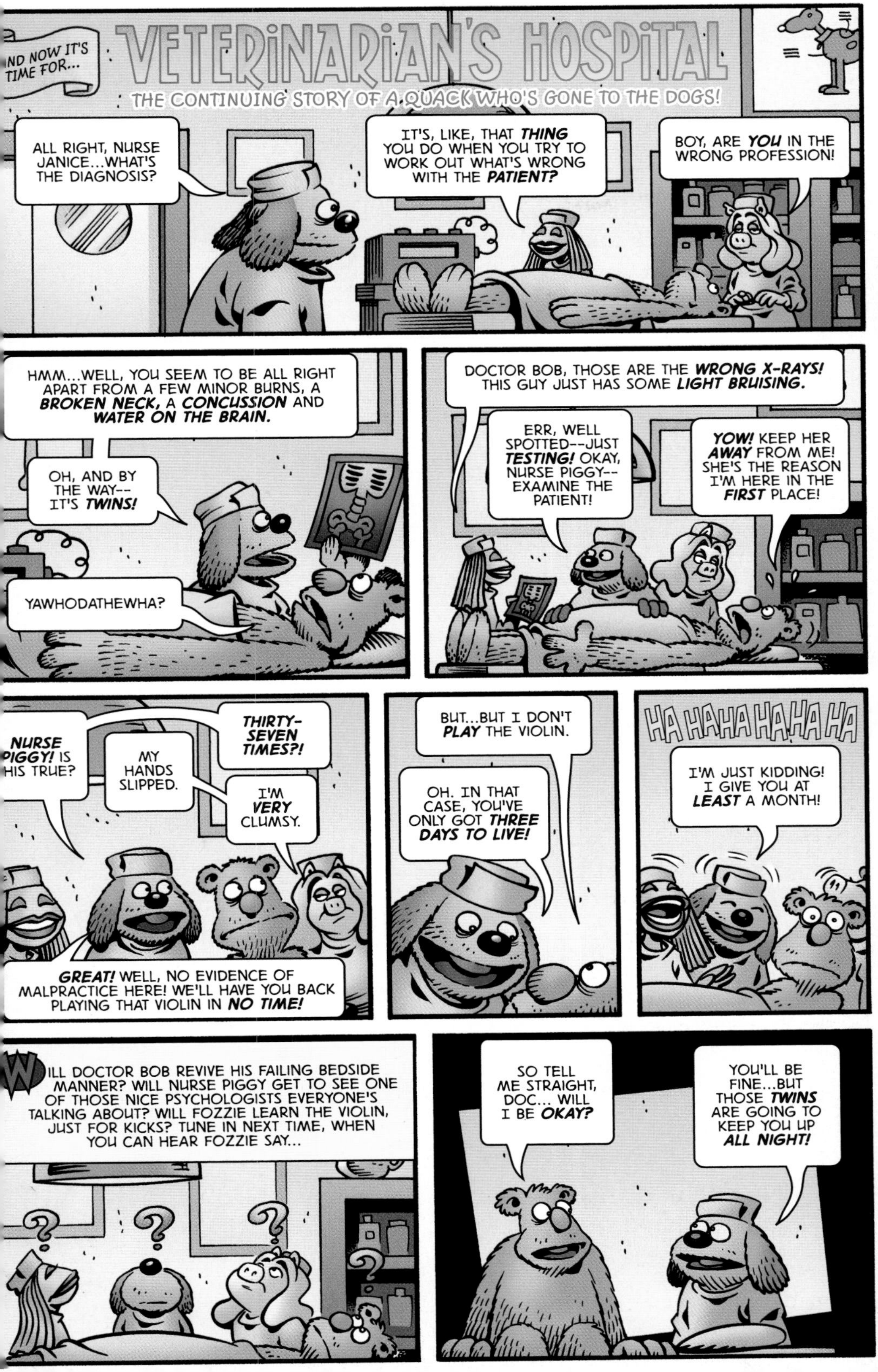
ND NOW IT'S TIME FOR...
VETERINARIAN'S HOSPITAL
THE CONTINUING STORY OF A QUACK WHO'S GONE TO THE DOGS!
ALL RIGHT, NURSE JANICE...WHAT'S THE DIAGNOSIS?
IT'S, LIKE, THAT THING YOU DO WHEN YOU TRY TO WORK OUT WHAT'S WRONG WITH THE PATIENT?
BOY, ARE YOU IN THE WRONG PROFESSION!
HMM...WELL, YOU SEEM TO BE ALL RIGHT APART FROM A FEW MINOR BURNS, A BROKEN NECK, A CONCUSSION AND WATER ON THE BRAIN.
OH, AND BY THE WAY-- IT'S TWINS!
YAWHODATHEWHA?
DOCTOR BOB, THOSE ARE THE WRONG X-RAYS! THIS GUY JUST HAS SOME LIGHT BRUISING.
ERR, WELL SPOTTED--JUST TESTING! OKAY, NURSE PIGGY-- EXAMINE THE PATIENT!
YOW! KEEP HER AWAY FROM ME! SHE'S THE REASON I'M HERE IN THE FIRST PLACE!
NURSE PIGGY! IS HIS TRUE?
MY HANDS SLIPPED.
THIRTY-SEVEN TIMES?!
I'M VERY CLUMSY.
GREAT! WELL, NO EVIDENCE OF MALPRACTICE HERE! WE'LL HAVE YOU BACK PLAYING THAT VIOLIN IN NO TIME!
BUT...BUT I DON'T PLAY THE VIOLIN.
OH. IN THAT CASE, YOU'VE ONLY GOT THREE DAYS TO LIVE!
HA HAHA HAHA HA
I'M JUST KIDDING! I GIVE YOU AT LEAST A MONTH!
WILL DOCTOR BOB REVIVE HIS FAILING BEDSIDE MANNER? WILL NURSE PIGGY GET TO SEE ONE OF THOSE NICE PSYCHOLOGISTS EVERYONE'S TALKING ABOUT? WILL FOZZIE LEARN THE VIOLIN, JUST FOR KICKS? TUNE IN NEXT TIME, WHEN YOU CAN HEAR FOZZIE SAY...
SO TELL ME STRAIGHT, DOC... WILL I BE OKAY?
YOU'LL BE FINE...BUT THOSE TWINS ARE GOING TO KEEP YOU UP ALL NIGHT!

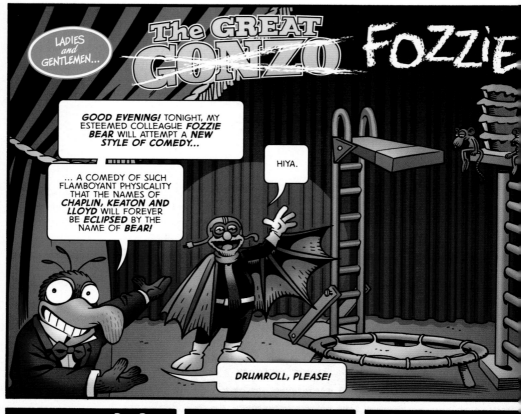

LADIES and GENTLEMEN...

The GREAT ~~GONZO~~ FOZZIE

GOOD EVENING! TONIGHT, MY ESTEEMED COLLEAGUE *FOZZIE BEAR* WILL ATTEMPT A *NEW STYLE OF COMEDY...*

... A COMEDY OF SUCH FLAMBOYANT PHYSICALITY THAT THE NAMES OF *CHAPLIN, KEATON AND LLOYD* WILL FOREVER BE *ECLIPSED* BY THE NAME OF *BEAR!*

HIYA.

DRUMROLL, PLEASE!

DURRRUDUDUDUDURUDUDUDUDUDU

P-TSHH

DUGADUGADUGAD

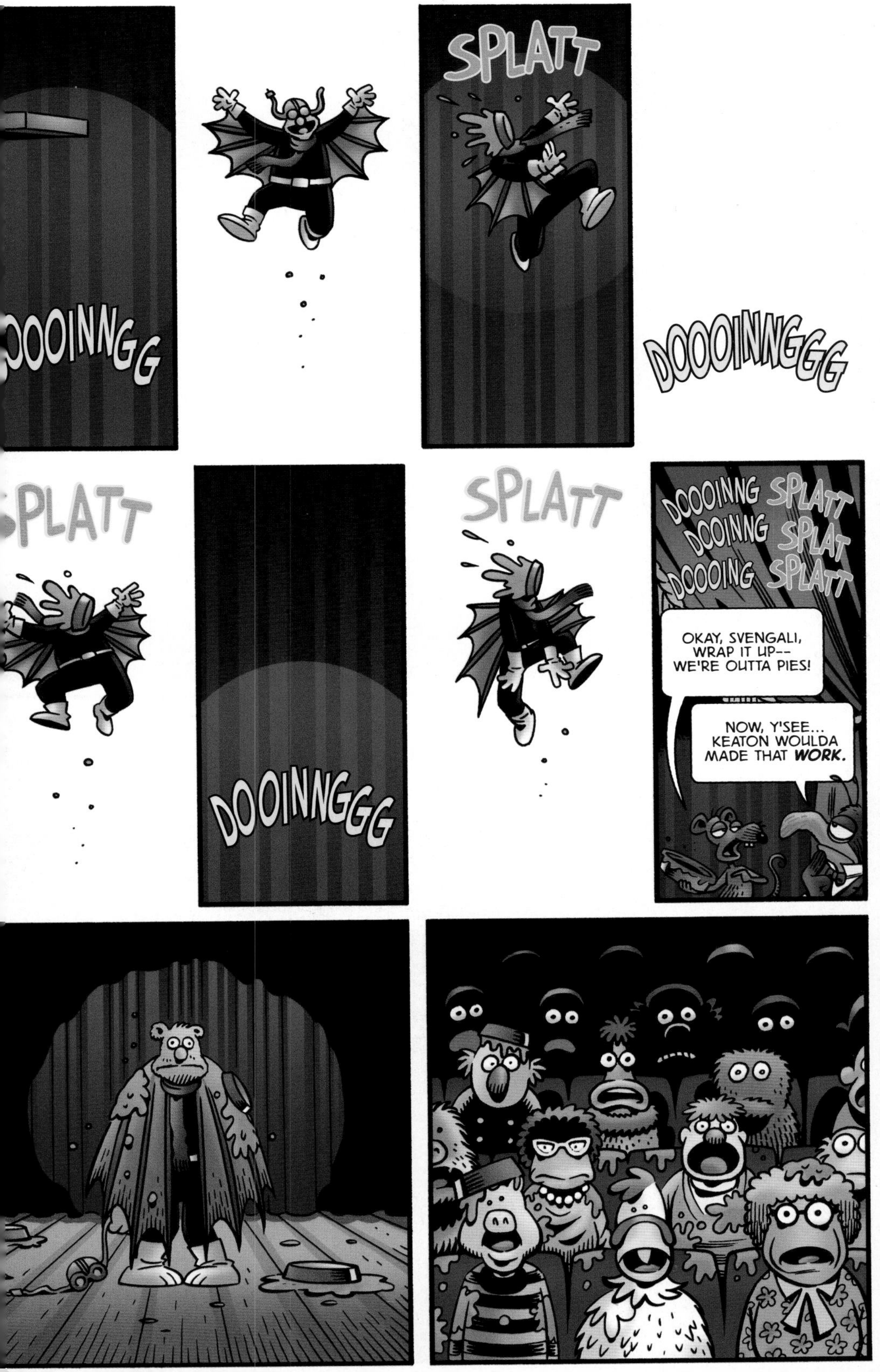

DOOOINNGG
SPLATT
DOOOINNGGG
SPLATT
DOOINNGGG
SPLATT
DOOOINNG SPLATT
DOOINNG SPLAT
DOOOING SPLATT
OKAY, SVENGALI, WRAP IT UP-- WE'RE OUTTA PIES!
NOW, Y'SEE... KEATON WOULDA MADE THAT **WORK.**

HEY, FOZZIE. M'MAN. I HAVEN'T SEEN A FACE SO LONG SINCE WE HAD *SPARKY THE WONDER HORSE* ON THE SHOW.

AAAUGHH! I WAS GOING TO GO *BEATNIK STYLE* FOR MY NEXT BIT, BUT I DON'T KNOW IF I CAN *FACE IT!* I KEEP GETTING *HURT* OR *BOOED OFF STAGE*--OR *BOTH!*

HMM... TRICKY.

IT'S JUST...I DON'T KNOW WHAT I'M DOING *WRONG!* I DON'T KNOW WHAT THEY *WANT* FROM ME! I SHOULD COME ON AND GO BLABLABL AND THEY'RE SUPPOSED TO *ROLL IN THE AISLES!*

WELL, IT'S TOUGH ALL OVER...

WELL, *SURE.* BUT I DON'T UNDERSTAND HOW *LOOKING TO THE PAST* COULD *FAIL!*

YOU KNOW, IT'S USUALLY A GOOD IDEA JUST TO BE YOURSELF.

"BEING MYSELF" IS WHAT GOT ME INTO TROUBLE IN THE *FIRST* PLACE!

NO, I'VE BEEN LOOKING AT THIS ALL *WRONG!* MY HEROES DIDN'T LOOK *BACKWARDS* ALL THE TIME! THEY WERE GREAT BECAUSE THEY WEREN'T AFRAID OF THE *NEW...* THE *BOLD...*THE *DIFFERENT!*

ROWLF...*THANK YOU!* NOW I KNOW WHAT I HAVE TO DO! I *OWE* YOU ONE, OLD PAL!

SURE, NO PROBLEM. GLAD IT WORKED OUT!

I SAY THE SAME THING TO EVERYONE. FUNNY HOW IT WORKS EVERY TIME.

HMM—TRICKY
WELL, IT'S TOUGH ALL OVER
BE YOURSELF

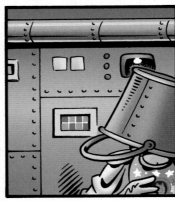

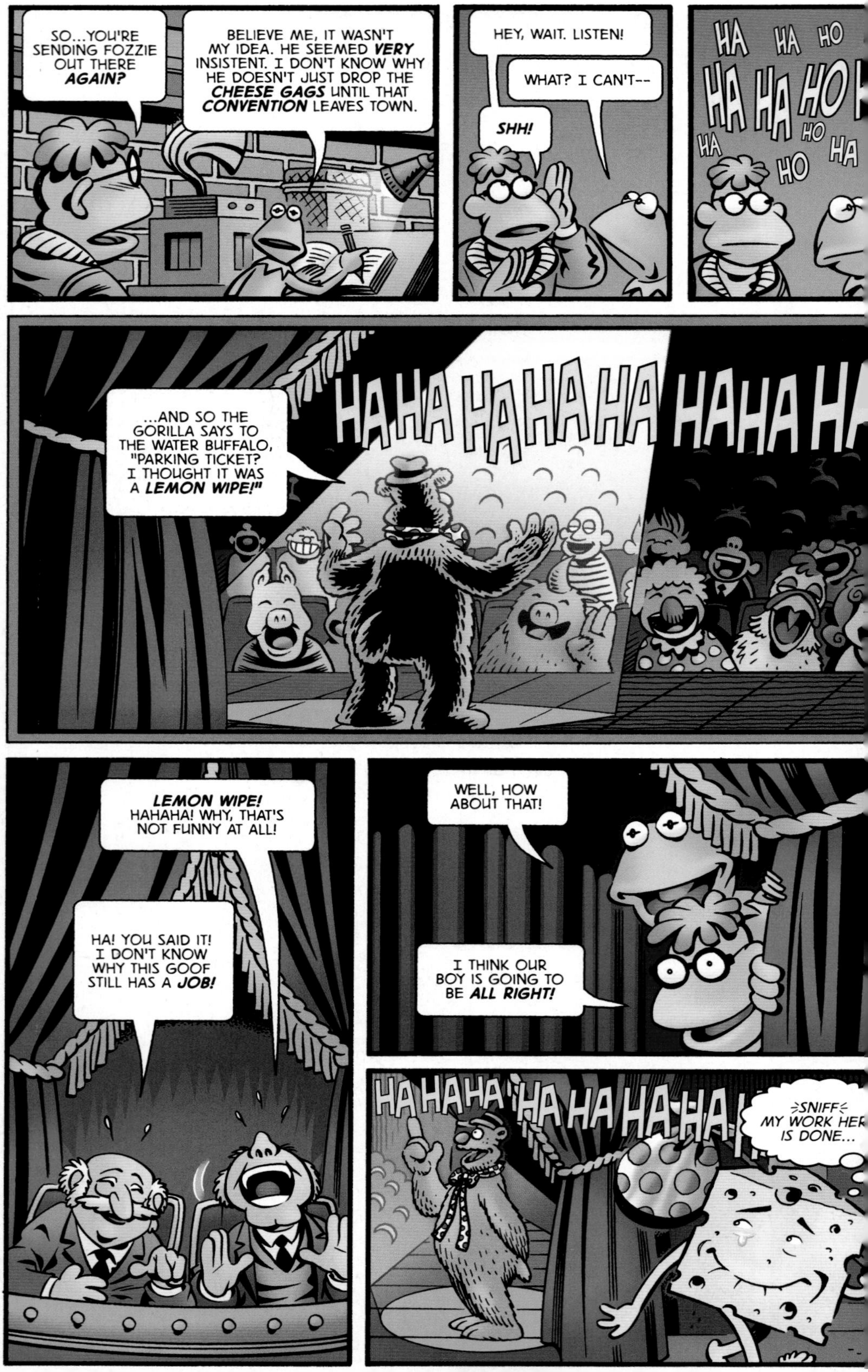

SO...YOU'RE SENDING FOZZIE OUT THERE AGAIN?
BELIEVE ME, IT WASN'T MY IDEA. HE SEEMED VERY INSISTENT. I DON'T KNOW WHY HE DOESN'T JUST DROP THE CHEESE GAGS UNTIL THAT CONVENTION LEAVES TOWN.
HEY, WAIT. LISTEN!
WHAT? I CAN'T--
SHH!
HA HA HO
HA HA HO
HA HO HA
HO
HAHA HAHAHA HAHAHA
...AND SO THE GORILLA SAYS TO THE WATER BUFFALO, "PARKING TICKET? I THOUGHT IT WAS A LEMON WIPE!"
LEMON WIPE! HAHAHA! WHY, THAT'S NOT FUNNY AT ALL!
HA! YOU SAID IT! I DON'T KNOW WHY THIS GOOF STILL HAS A JOB!
WELL, HOW ABOUT THAT!
I THINK OUR BOY IS GOING TO BE ALL RIGHT!
HAHAHA HA HA HA HA
SNIFF
MY WORK HER
IS DONE...

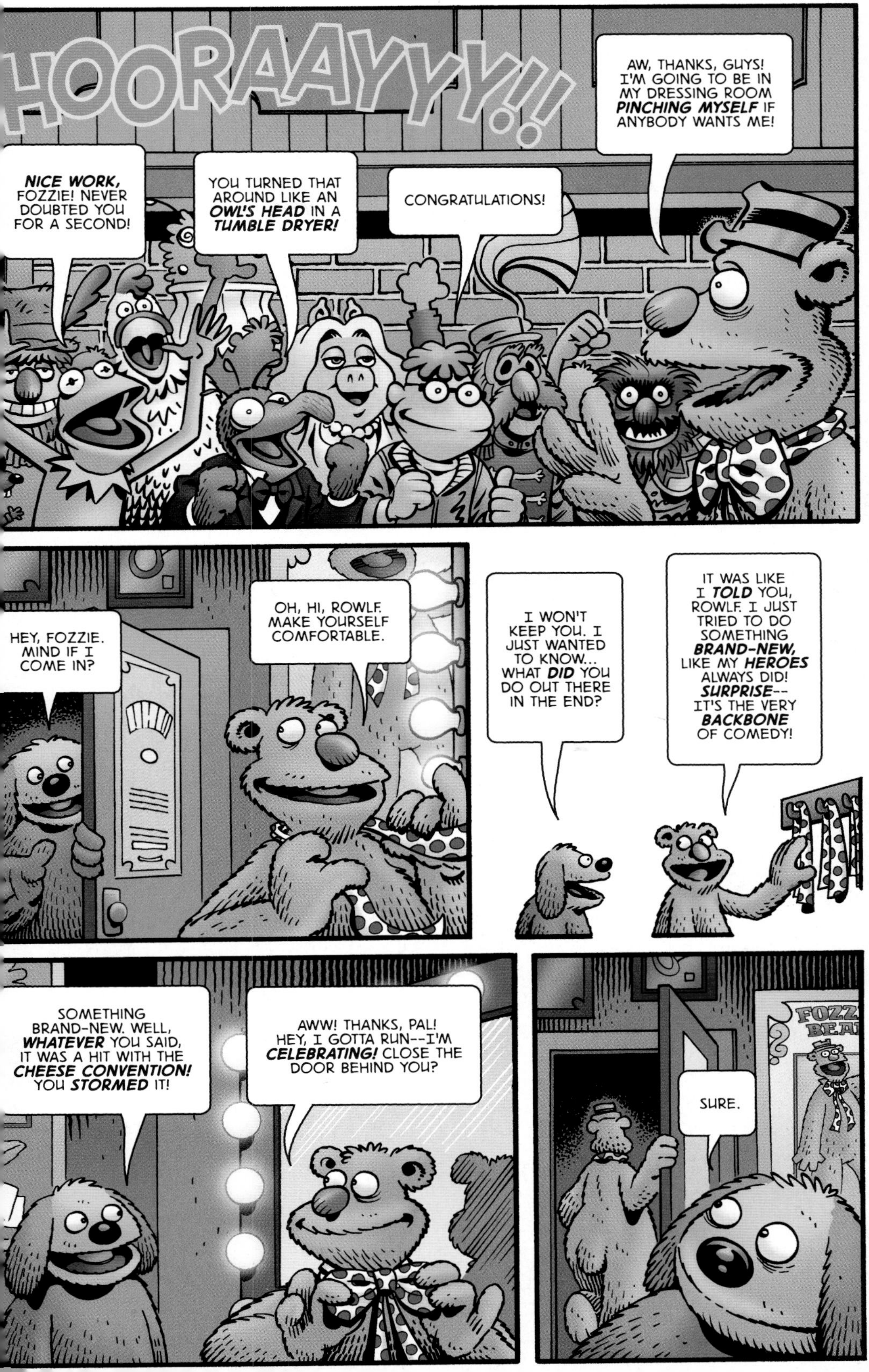
HOORAAYYY!!
AW, THANKS, GUYS! I'M GOING TO BE IN MY DRESSING ROOM PINCHING MYSELF IF ANYBODY WANTS ME!
NICE WORK, FOZZIE! NEVER DOUBTED YOU FOR A SECOND!
YOU TURNED THAT AROUND LIKE AN OWL'S HEAD IN A TUMBLE DRYER!
CONGRATULATIONS!
HEY, FOZZIE. MIND IF I COME IN?
OH, HI, ROWLF. MAKE YOURSELF COMFORTABLE.
I WON'T KEEP YOU. I JUST WANTED TO KNOW... WHAT DID YOU DO OUT THERE IN THE END?
IT WAS LIKE I TOLD YOU, ROWLF. I JUST TRIED TO DO SOMETHING BRAND-NEW, LIKE MY HEROES ALWAYS DID! SURPRISE-- IT'S THE VERY BACKBONE OF COMEDY!
SOMETHING BRAND-NEW. WELL, WHATEVER YOU SAID, IT WAS A HIT WITH THE CHEESE CONVENTION! YOU STORMED IT!
AWW! THANKS, PAL! HEY, I GOTTA RUN--I'M CELEBRATING! CLOSE THE DOOR BEHIND YOU?
SURE.

FOZZIE'S SCRIPT! I'VE JUST *GOT* TO KNOW!

Script

So the dodo says to the zebra, "I'd like some ~~cheese~~ milk please." And the zebra says, "~~Cheese~~ Milk? I thought it was a sub-cutaneous discharge!" So ~~dr~~ goes, "Phew! That relief! I'm not ~~a doctor, I run~~ I'm a milk ma from ~~cheese shop in Des~~ ines!" But ~~cheese~~ milk funny business...

WELL, I'LL BE HORNSWAGGLED! LOOKS LIKE FOZZIE DECIDED TO *BE HIMSELF* AFTER ALL...AND IT *WORKED,* TOO!

HMMM...I WONDER IF I SHOULD TELL HIM ABOUT THE DAIRY FARMERS' CONVENTION NEXT WEEK...?

FOZZ BEA

THE FUNNIES IN THE WO

The En

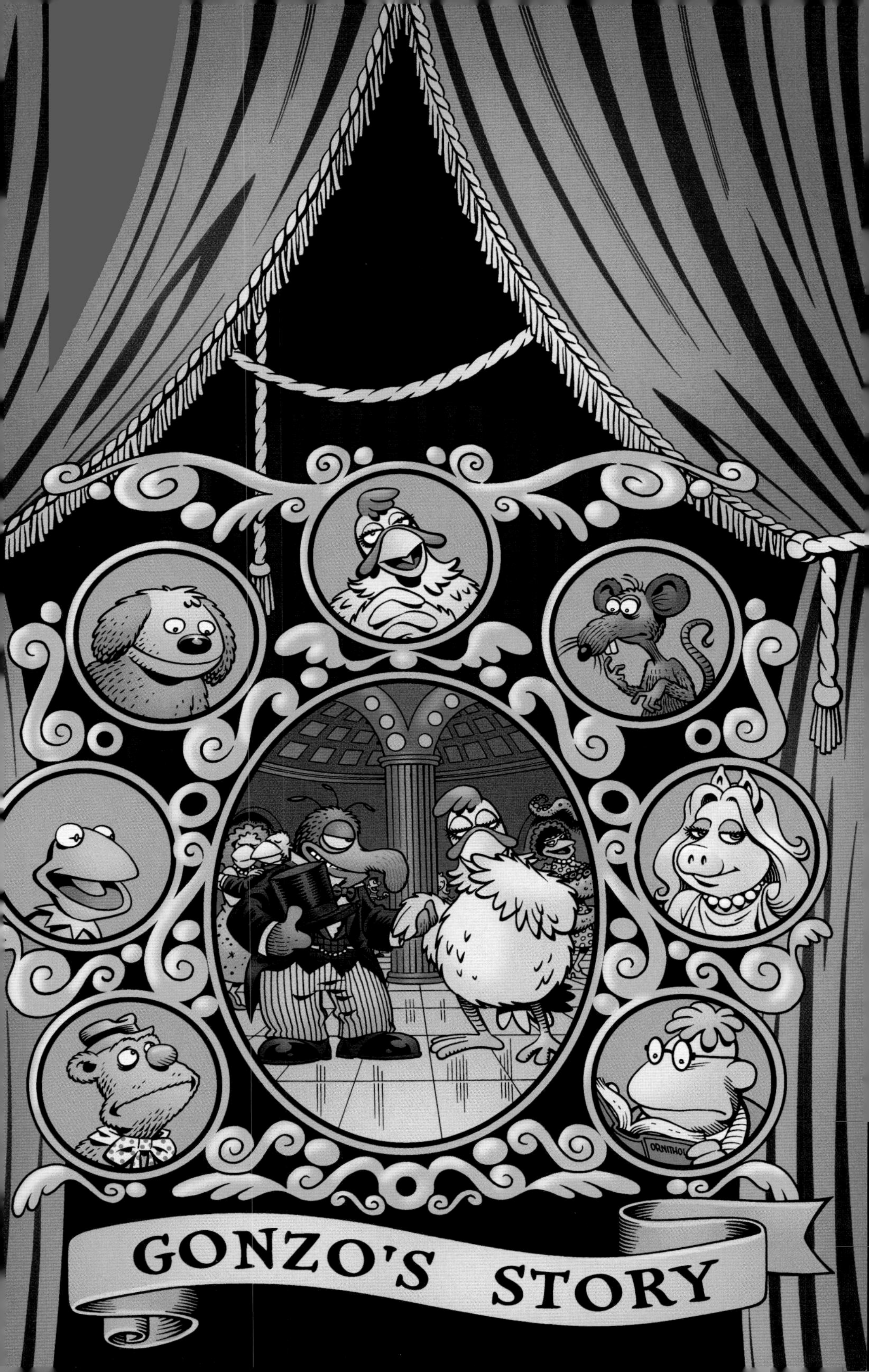
ORNITHOL
GONZO'S STORY

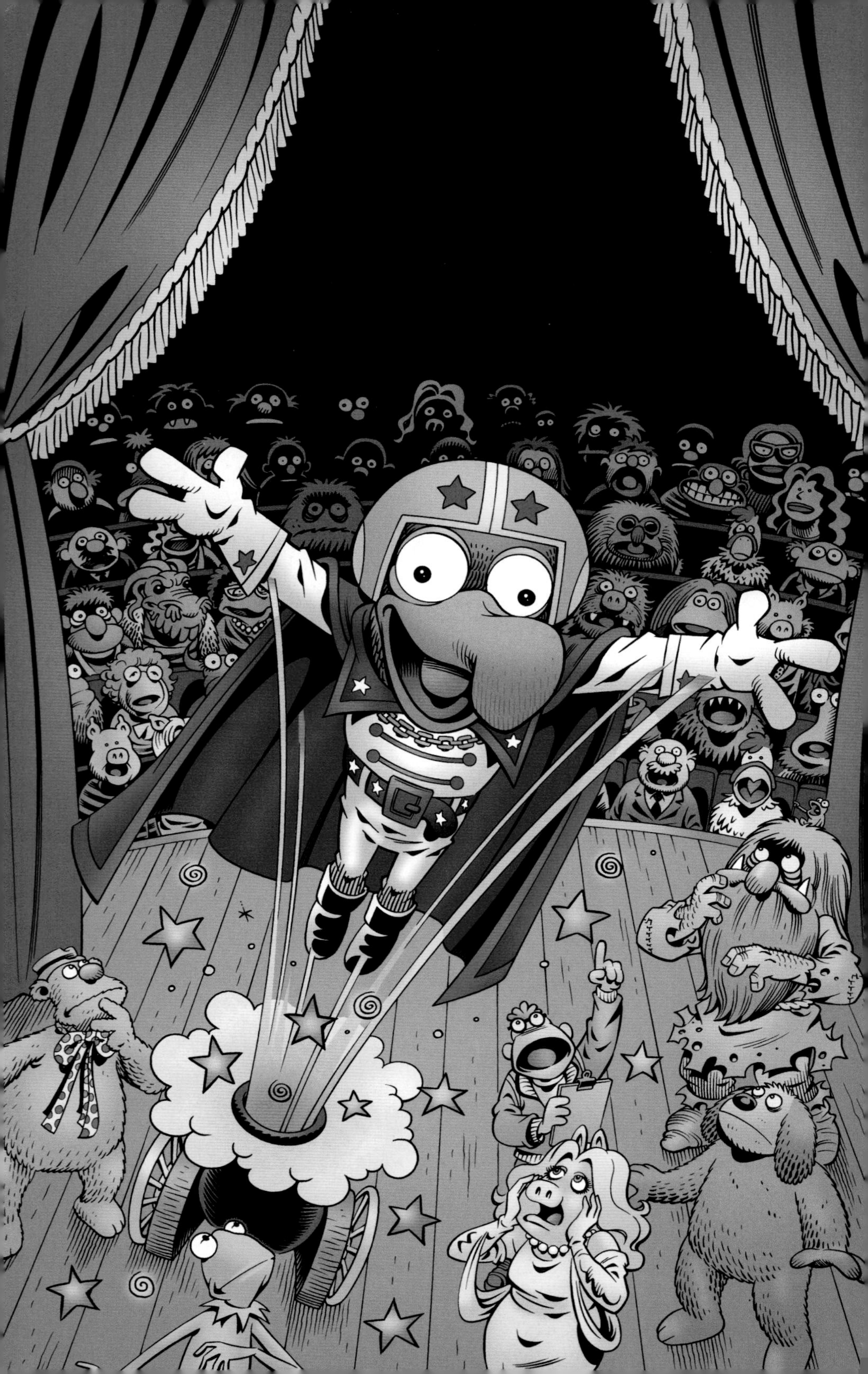

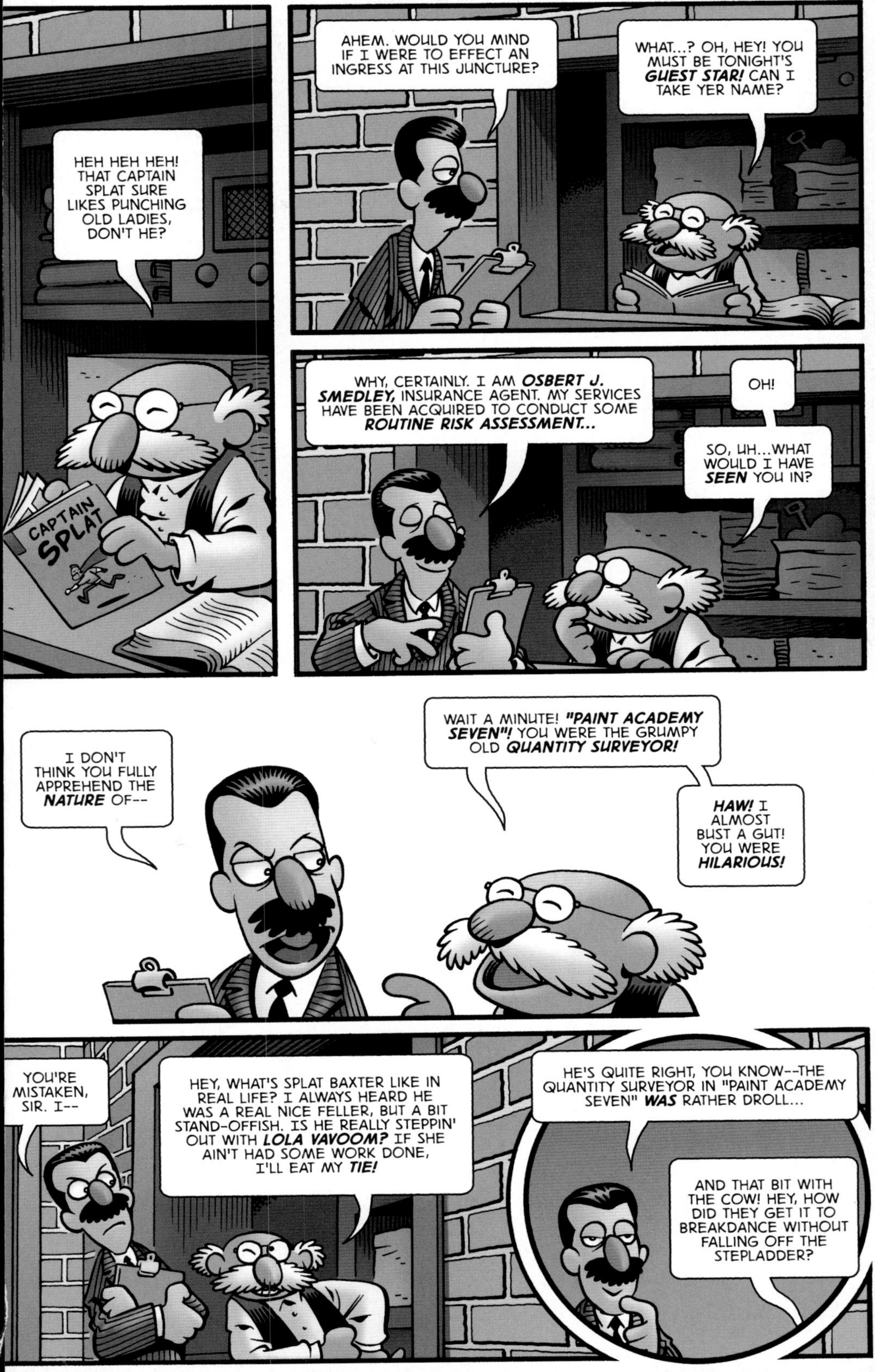
HEH HEH HEH! THAT CAPTAIN SPLAT SURE LIKES PUNCHING OLD LADIES, DON'T HE?
AHEM. WOULD YOU MIND IF I WERE TO EFFECT AN INGRESS AT THIS JUNCTURE?
WHAT...? OH, HEY! YOU MUST BE TONIGHT'S GUEST STAR! CAN I TAKE YER NAME?
CAPTAIN SPLAT
WHY, CERTAINLY. I AM OSBERT J. SMEDLEY, INSURANCE AGENT. MY SERVICES HAVE BEEN ACQUIRED TO CONDUCT SOME ROUTINE RISK ASSESSMENT...
OH!
SO, UH...WHAT WOULD I HAVE SEEN YOU IN?
WAIT A MINUTE! "PAINT ACADEMY SEVEN"! YOU WERE THE GRUMPY OLD QUANTITY SURVEYOR!
I DON'T THINK YOU FULLY APPREHEND THE NATURE OF--
HAW! I ALMOST BUST A GUT! YOU WERE HILARIOUS!
YOU'RE MISTAKEN, SIR. I--
HEY, WHAT'S SPLAT BAXTER LIKE IN REAL LIFE? I ALWAYS HEARD HE WAS A REAL NICE FELLER, BUT A BIT STAND-OFFISH. IS HE REALLY STEPPIN' OUT WITH LOLA VAVOOM? IF SHE AIN'T HAD SOME WORK DONE, I'LL EAT MY TIE!
HE'S QUITE RIGHT, YOU KNOW--THE QUANTITY SURVEYOR IN "PAINT ACADEMY SEVEN" WAS RATHER DROLL...
AND THAT BIT WITH THE COW! HEY, HOW DID THEY GET IT TO BREAKDANCE WITHOUT FALLING OFF THE STEPLADDER?

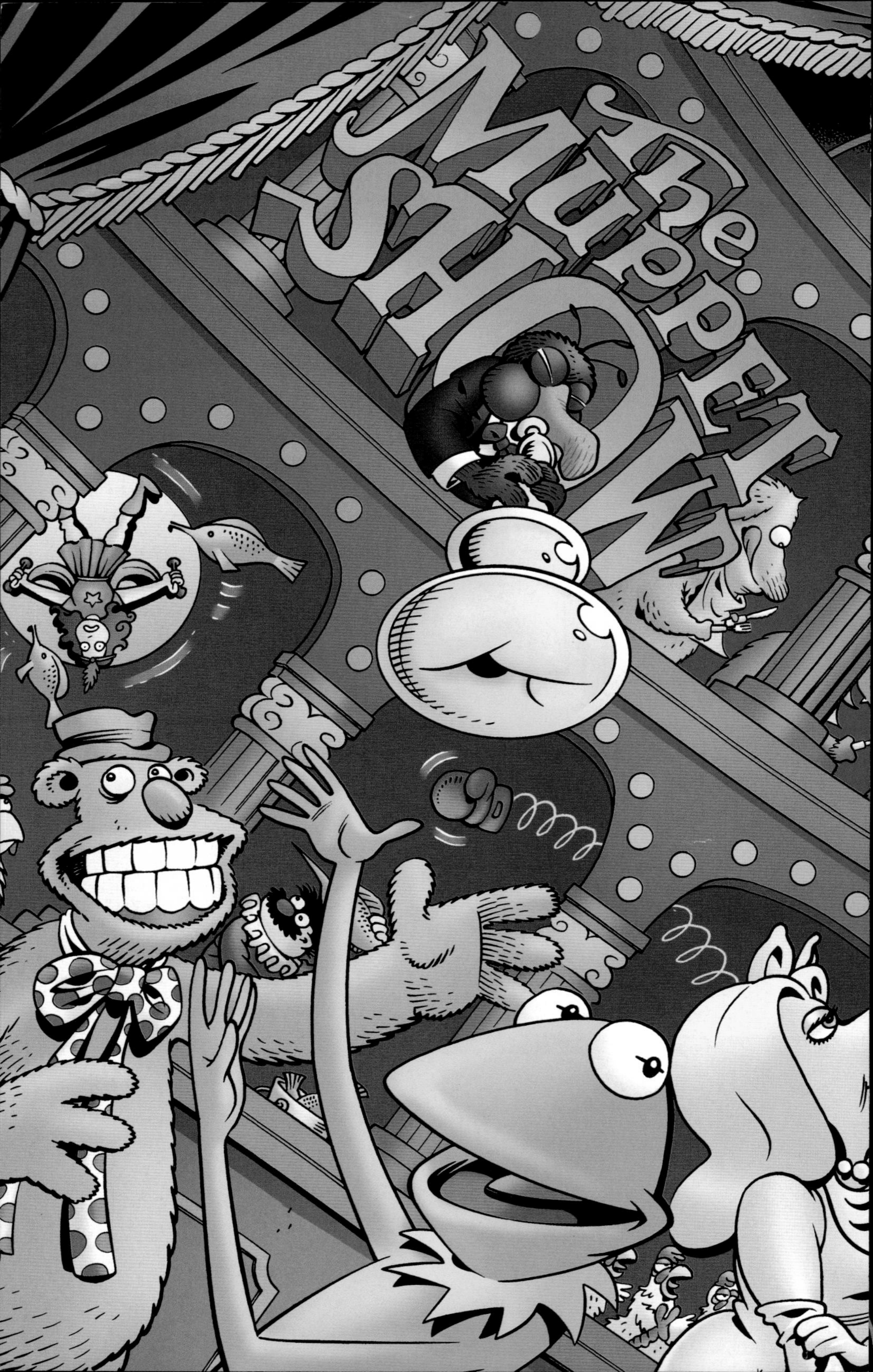
The Muppet SHOW

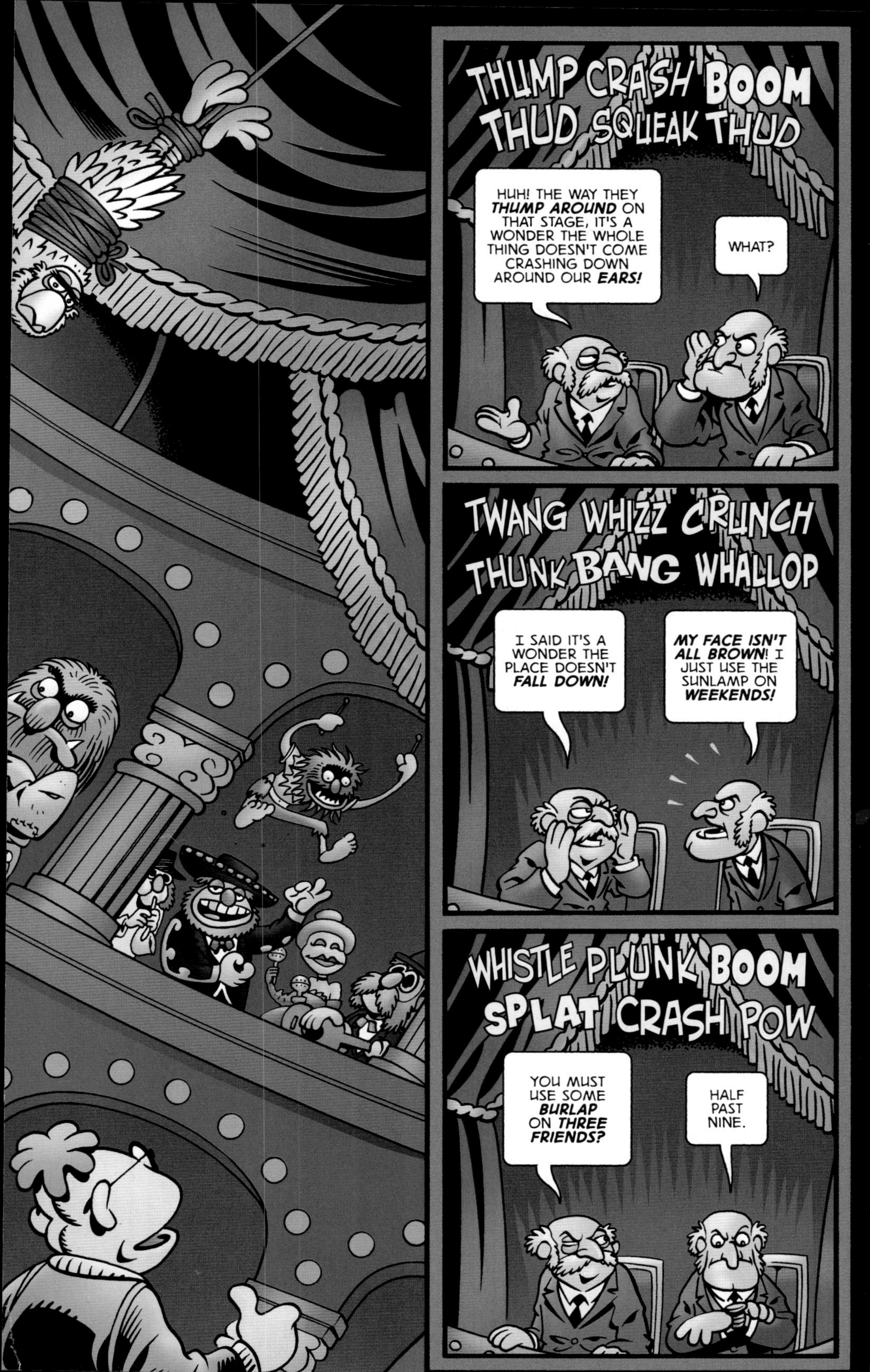
THUMP CRASH BOOM THUD SQUEAK THUD
HUH! THE WAY THEY THUMP AROUND ON THAT STAGE, IT'S A WONDER THE WHOLE THING DOESN'T COME CRASHING DOWN AROUND OUR EARS!
WHAT?
TWANG WHIZZ CRUNCH THUNK BANG WHALLOP
I SAID IT'S A WONDER THE PLACE DOESN'T FALL DOWN!
MY FACE ISN'T ALL BROWN! I JUST USE THE SUNLAMP ON WEEKENDS!
WHISTLE PLUNK BOOM SPLAT CRASH POW
YOU MUST USE SOME BURLAP ON THREE FRIENDS?
HALF PAST NINE.

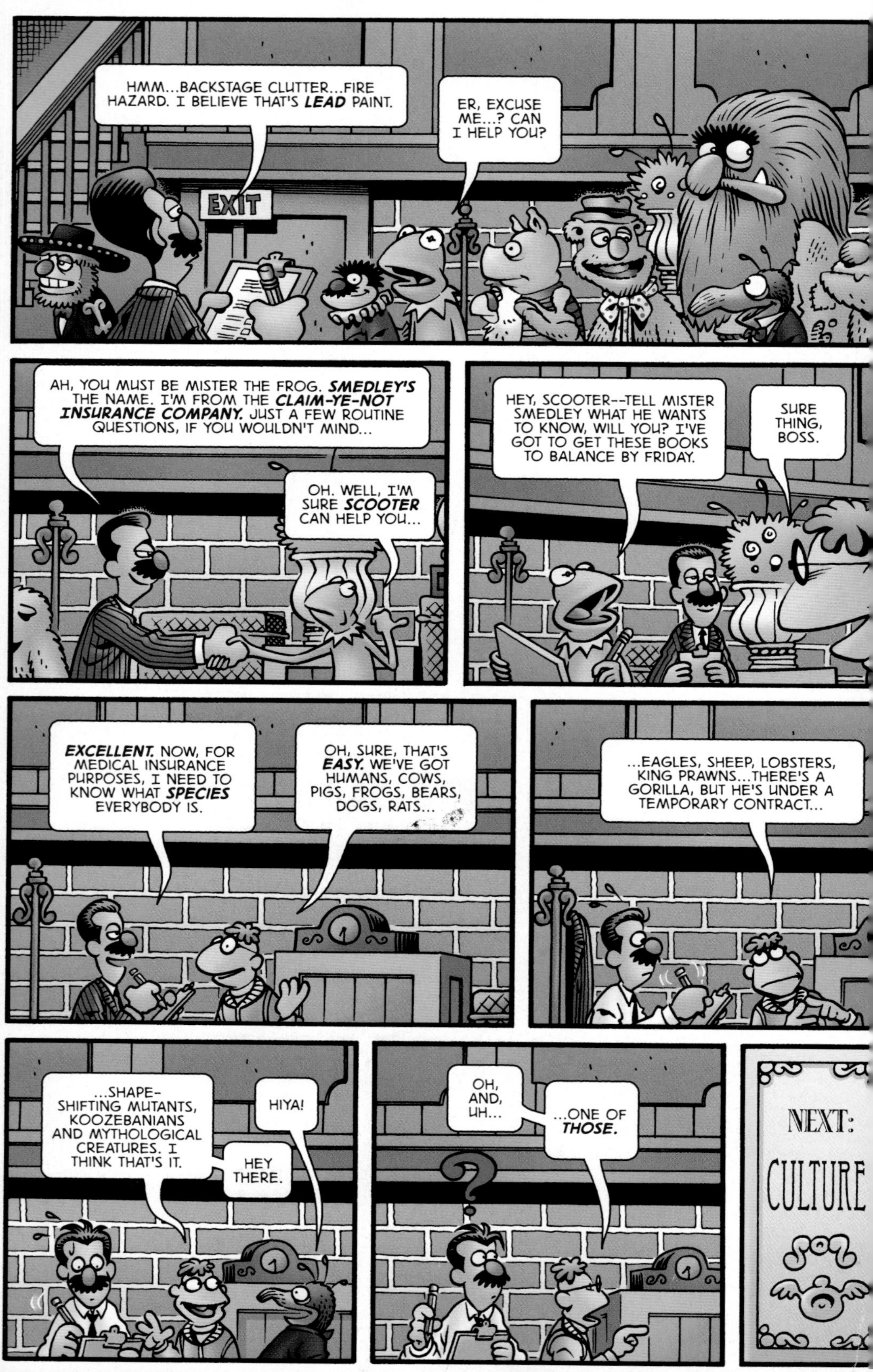
HMM...BACKSTAGE CLUTTER...FIRE HAZARD. I BELIEVE THAT'S LEAD PAINT.
EXIT
ER, EXCUSE ME...? CAN I HELP YOU?
AH, YOU MUST BE MISTER THE FROG. SMEDLEY'S THE NAME. I'M FROM THE CLAIM-YE-NOT INSURANCE COMPANY. JUST A FEW ROUTINE QUESTIONS, IF YOU WOULDN'T MIND...
OH. WELL, I'M SURE SCOOTER CAN HELP YOU...
HEY, SCOOTER--TELL MISTER SMEDLEY WHAT HE WANTS TO KNOW, WILL YOU? I'VE GOT TO GET THESE BOOKS TO BALANCE BY FRIDAY.
SURE THING, BOSS.
EXCELLENT. NOW, FOR MEDICAL INSURANCE PURPOSES, I NEED TO KNOW WHAT SPECIES EVERYBODY IS.
OH, SURE, THAT'S EASY. WE'VE GOT HUMANS, COWS, PIGS, FROGS, BEARS, DOGS, RATS...
...EAGLES, SHEEP, LOBSTERS, KING PRAWNS...THERE'S A GORILLA, BUT HE'S UNDER A TEMPORARY CONTRACT...
...SHAPE-SHIFTING MUTANTS, KOOZEBANIANS AND MYTHOLOGICAL CREATURES. I THINK THAT'S IT.
HIYA!
HEY THERE.
OH, AND, UH...
...ONE OF THOSE.
NEXT:
CULTURE

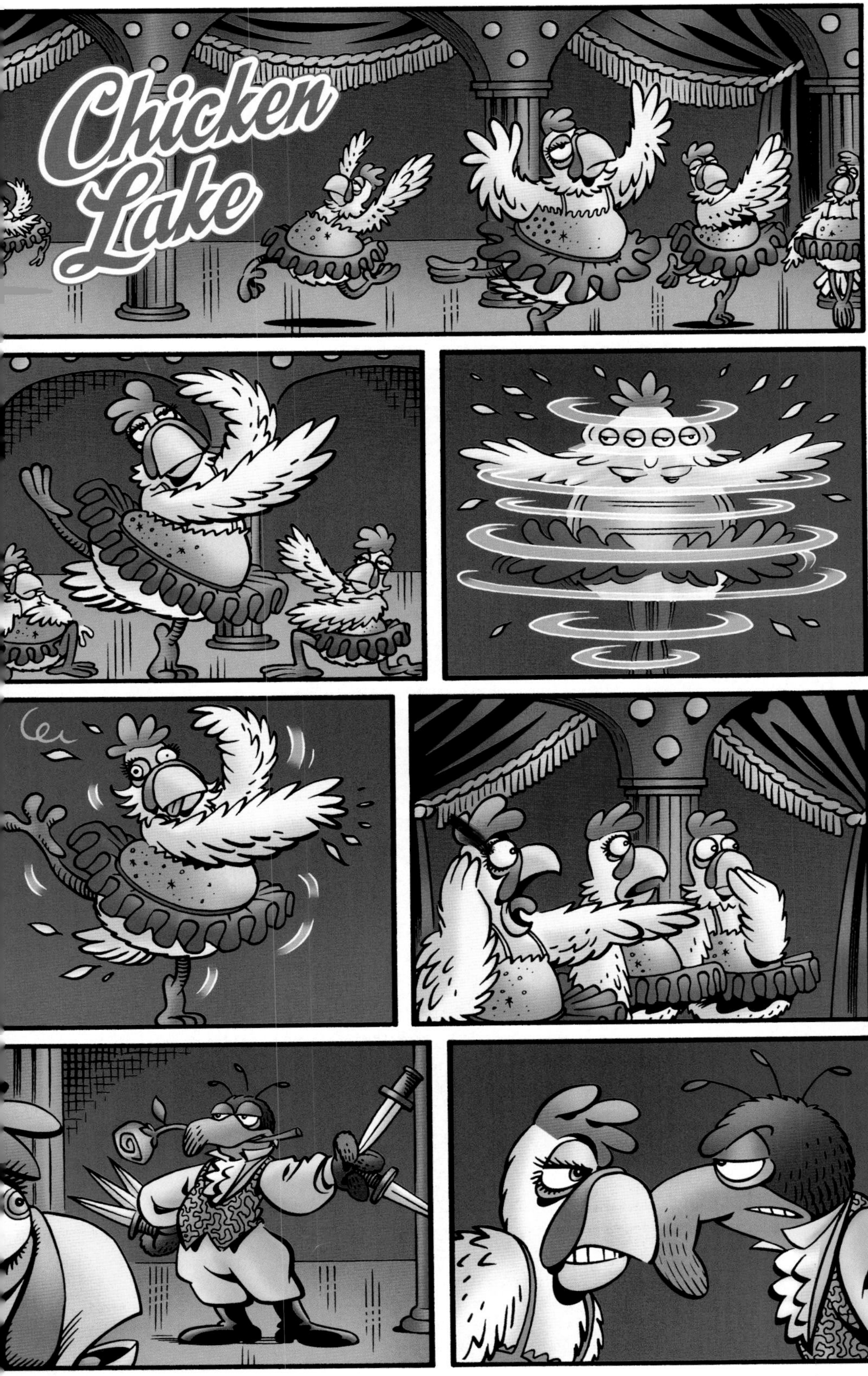
Chicken Lake

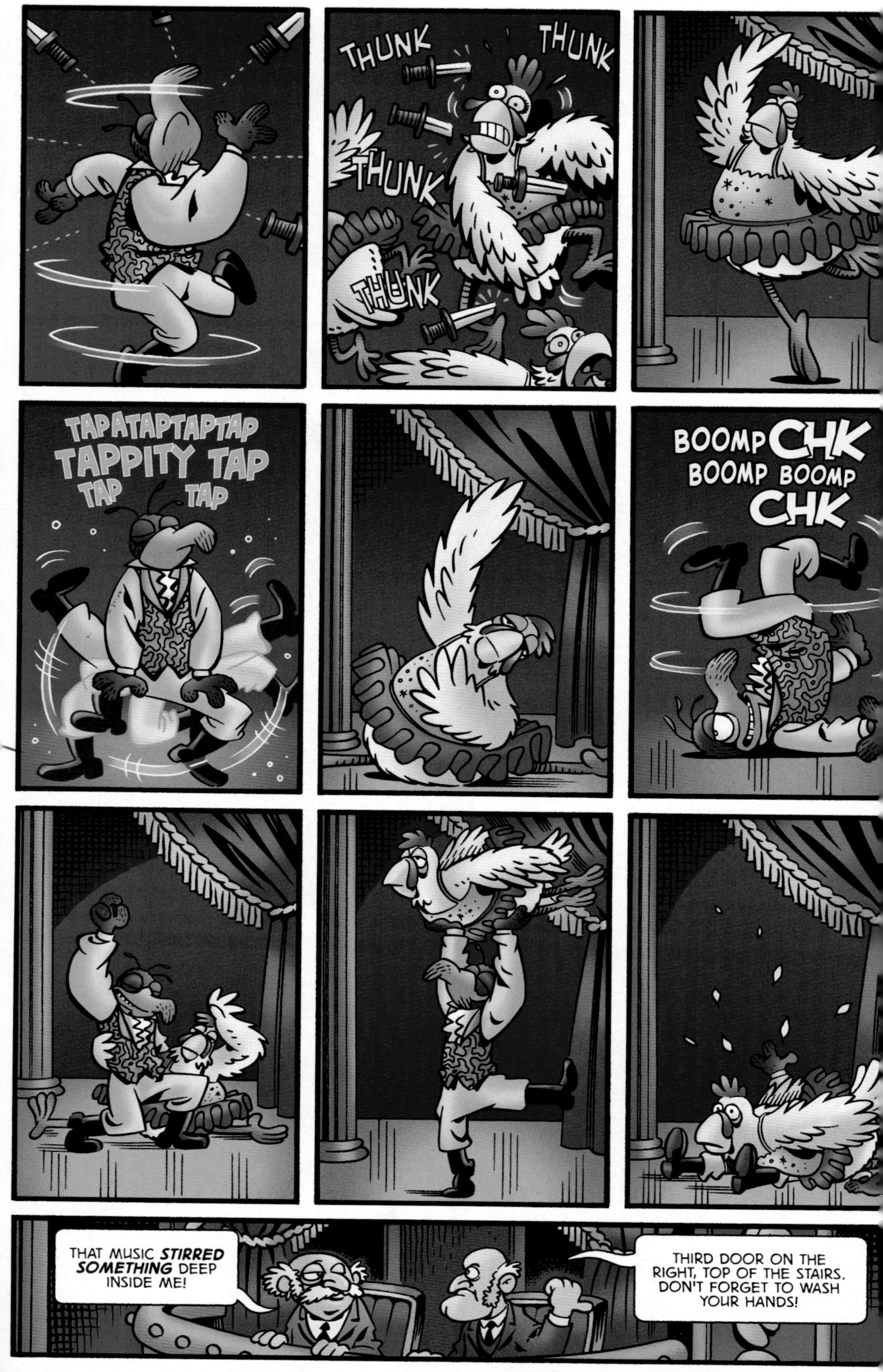
THUNK
THUNK
THUNK
THUNK
TAPATAPTAPTAP
TAPPITY TAP
TAP
TAP
BOOMP CHK
BOOMP BOOMP
CHK
THAT MUSIC **STIRRED SOMETHING** DEEP INSIDE ME!
THIRD DOOR ON THE RIGHT, TOP OF THE STAIRS. DON'T FORGET TO WASH YOUR HANDS!

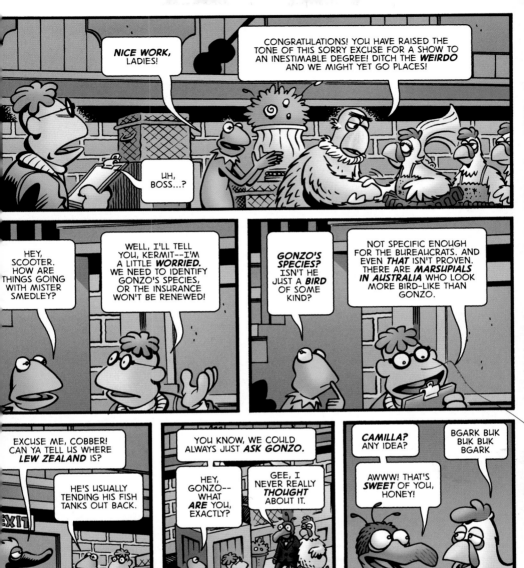

NICE WORK, LADIES!

CONGRATULATIONS! YOU HAVE RAISED THE TONE OF THIS SORRY EXCUSE FOR A SHOW TO AN INESTIMABLE DEGREE! DITCH THE *WEIRDO* AND WE MIGHT YET GO PLACES!

UH, BOSS...?

HEY, SCOOTER. HOW ARE THINGS GOING WITH MISTER SMEDLEY?

WELL, I'LL TELL YOU, KERMIT--I'M A LITTLE *WORRIED.* WE NEED TO IDENTIFY GONZO'S SPECIES, OR THE INSURANCE WON'T BE RENEWED!

GONZO'S SPECIES? ISN'T HE JUST A *BIRD* OF SOME KIND?

NOT SPECIFIC ENOUGH FOR THE BUREAUCRATS. AND EVEN *THAT* ISN'T PROVEN. THERE ARE *MARSUPIALS IN AUSTRALIA* WHO LOOK MORE BIRD-LIKE THAN GONZO.

EXCUSE ME, COBBER! CAN YA TELL US WHERE *LEW ZEALAND* IS?

HE'S USUALLY TENDING HIS FISH TANKS OUT BACK.

SWEET AS, MATE.

YOU KNOW, WE COULD ALWAYS JUST *ASK GONZO.*

HEY, GONZO-- WHAT *ARE* YOU, EXACTLY?

GEE, I NEVER REALLY *THOUGHT* ABOUT IT.

WELL, DOES ANYONE *ELSE* KNOW?

CAMILLA? ANY IDEA?

AWWW! THAT'S *SWEET* OF YOU, HONEY!

BGARK BUK BUK BUK BGARK

WHAT DID SHE SAY? *WHAT DID SHE SAY?*

SHE SAID I'LL ALWAYS BE A *CHICKEN* TO HER! ISN'T THAT *ADORABLE?*

YEAH. ADORABLE.

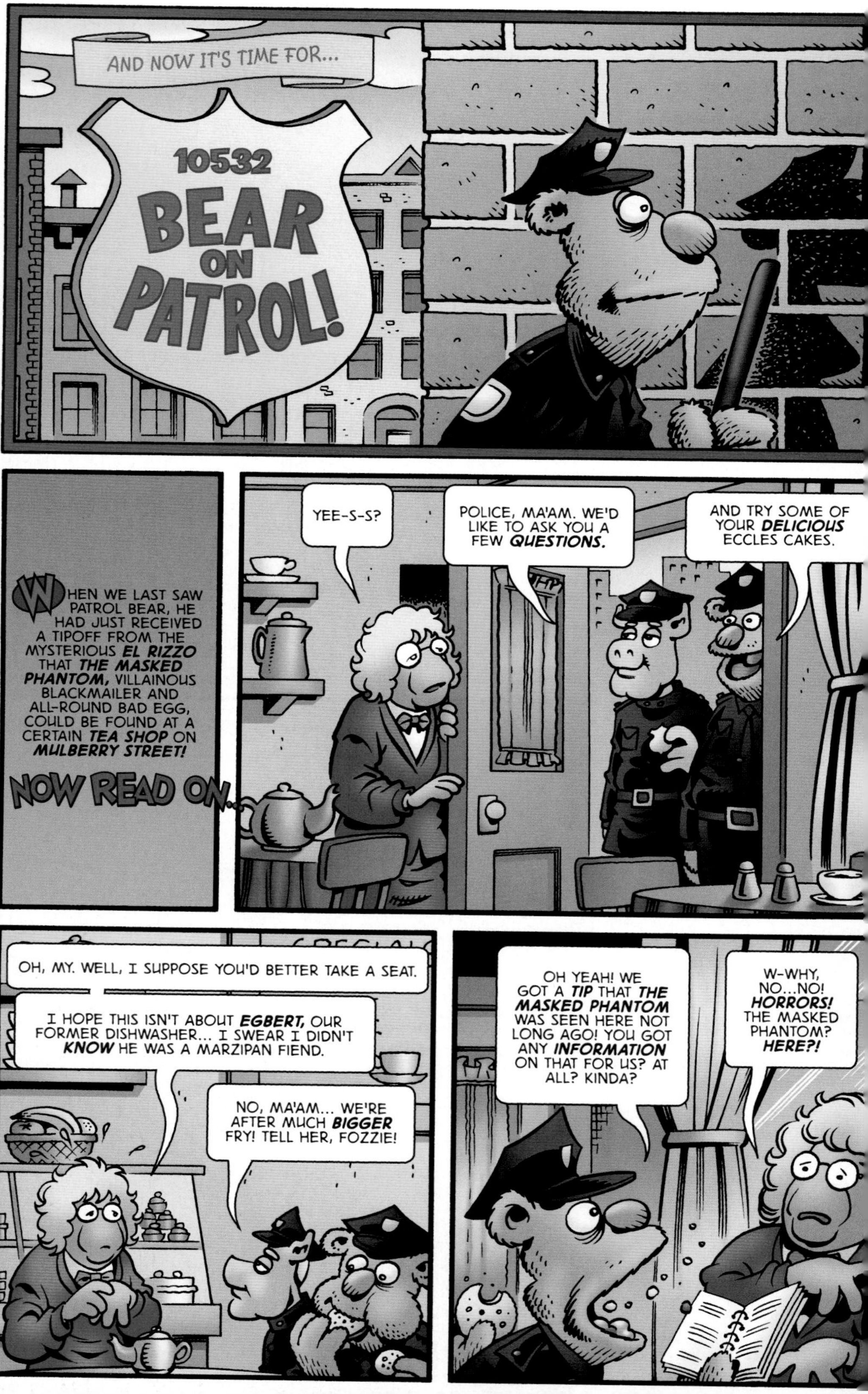
AND NOW IT'S TIME FOR...
10532
BEAR ON PATROL!
WHEN WE LAST SAW PATROL BEAR, HE HAD JUST RECEIVED A TIPOFF FROM THE MYSTERIOUS EL RIZZO THAT THE MASKED PHANTOM, VILLAINOUS BLACKMAILER AND ALL-ROUND BAD EGG, COULD BE FOUND AT A CERTAIN TEA SHOP ON MULBERRY STREET!
NOW READ ON...
YEE-S-S?
POLICE, MA'AM. WE'D LIKE TO ASK YOU A FEW QUESTIONS.
AND TRY SOME OF YOUR DELICIOUS ECCLES CAKES.
OH, MY. WELL, I SUPPOSE YOU'D BETTER TAKE A SEAT.
I HOPE THIS ISN'T ABOUT EGBERT, OUR FORMER DISHWASHER... I SWEAR I DIDN'T KNOW HE WAS A MARZIPAN FIEND.
NO, MA'AM... WE'RE AFTER MUCH BIGGER FRY! TELL HER, FOZZIE!
OH YEAH! WE GOT A TIP THAT THE MASKED PHANTOM WAS SEEN HERE NOT LONG AGO! YOU GOT ANY INFORMATION ON THAT FOR US? AT ALL? KINDA?
W-WHY, NO...NO! HORRORS! THE MASKED PHANTOM? HERE?!

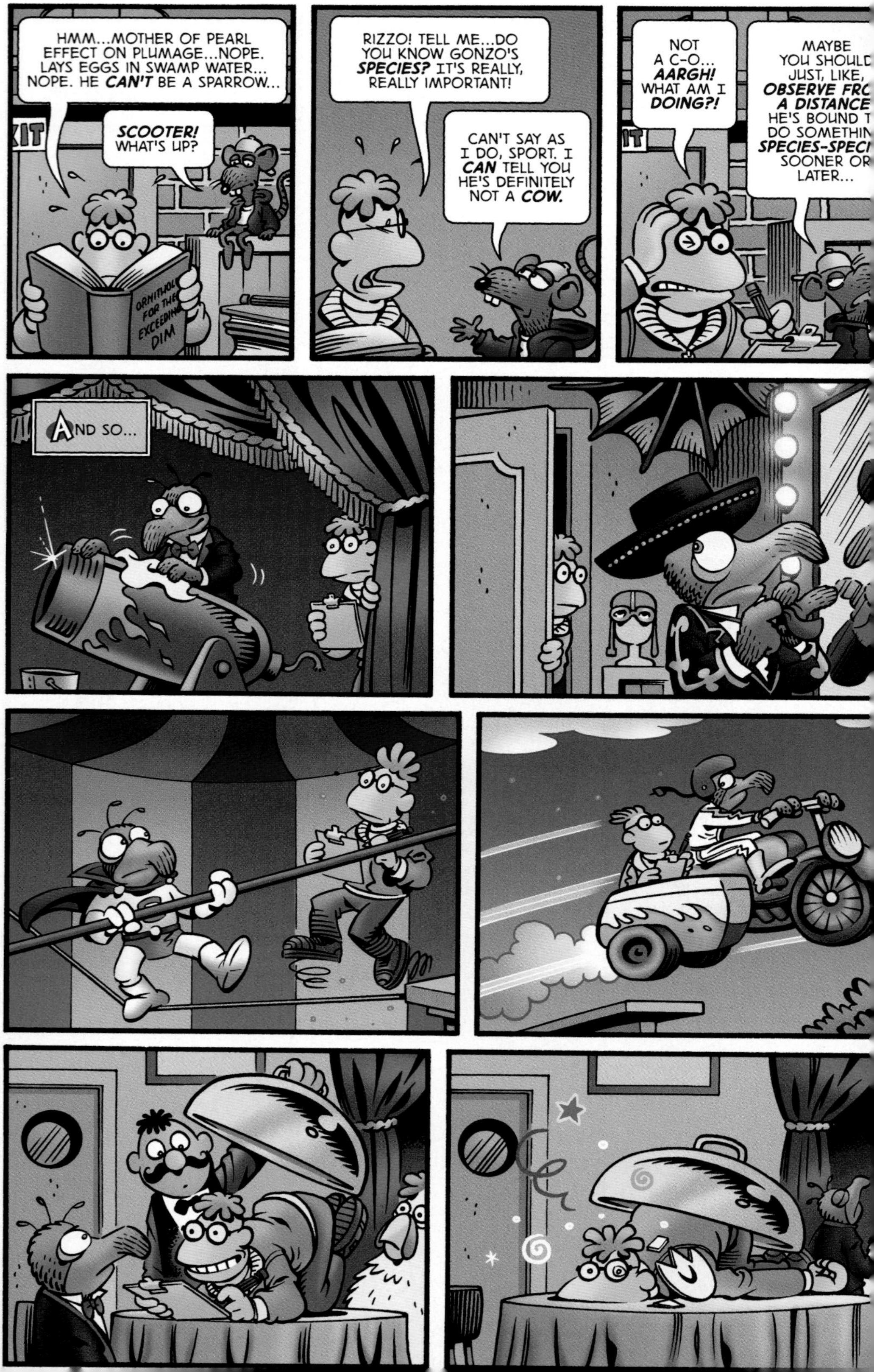
HMM...MOTHER OF PEARL EFFECT ON PLUMAGE...NOPE. LAYS EGGS IN SWAMP WATER... NOPE. HE CAN'T BE A SPARROW...
SCOOTER! WHAT'S UP?
ORNITHOLO... FOR THE EXCEEDING DIM
RIZZO! TELL ME...DO YOU KNOW GONZO'S SPECIES? IT'S REALLY, REALLY IMPORTANT!
CAN'T SAY AS I DO, SPORT. I CAN TELL YOU HE'S DEFINITELY NOT A COW.
NOT A C-O... AARGH! WHAT AM I DOING?!
MAYBE YOU SHOULD JUST, LIKE, OBSERVE FRO A DISTANCE HE'S BOUND T DO SOMETHIN SPECIES-SPECI SOONER OR LATER...
AND SO...

OKAY...THIS DOESN'T ADD UP AT **ALL.**

HE **CAN'T** BE A DODO. I'M MISSING SOMETHING FUNDAMENTAL... BUT WHAT? **WHAT??**

CRESTED GRE~~CRESTED GRE~~
~~DUSKY WARBLE~~
~~LESSER-SPOTTED~~ ???

DODO
OSTRICH
PUKEKO

TIME TO TRY A **DIFFERENT TACK!** MAYBE I CAN APPROACH THIS BY **CONSENSUS!**

...HAT DO *YOU* THINK GONZO IS?

I ALWAYS THOUGHT HE WAS SOME KIND OF **ANTEATER.**

CLEARLY THE RESULT OF **SCIENCE GONE MAD!**

NOT THAT WE SCIENTISTS **GO** MAD, YOU UNDERSTAND.

HOËR BÜRK DER ÜMLÄÜT ÜRN DER BOËKY-BOËK?

LOB-STER! LOB-STER! **AAAAHHH!**

MAN, HE CAN SWING **ANY** WHICH WAY...I CAN DIG IT.

I, FOR ONE, WOULD LIKE TO THINK OF HIM AS AN *HOMME TRÉS* GENTLE.

UNFORTUNATELY, HE'S TOO **WEIRD.**

MEEP! MEEP MEEP MEEP MEEP **MEEP!**

GONZO? IS HE THE GREEN FELLER WITH THE FLIPPERS OR THE HAIRY ONE IN THE HAT?

⇃SIGH⇂

What a day. Not only had my old partner Pyles set up a rival shop near my patch, he'd stolen my girl just to rub it in my face. And as if that weren't bad enough, I was down to my last few drops of Sarsaparilla.

Things weren't looking too good for...

FRIDAY
13
JUNE

GUMSHOE
McGURK,
PRIVATE EYE!

That's when **she** walked into my life.

B-B-BGARK!

HOT TAMALES!

BUK BUK BUK **BGARK!**

THE GOBSTOPPER RUBY? IT'S **PRICELESS!**

BRRRR BUK BUK BUK

WHAT DO YOU MEAN, **"GONE"?!**

BGARK BUK BUK **BGARK!**

BUT WASN'T IT **LOCKED?**

BGARK!!

Strange, indeed! If her story checked out, it would take all my facult⸺ and resources to recover that glitzy bauble. The question was, did ⸺ check out? Or was this just some flim flam to get me out of the wa⸺

I decided to play it cool.

OKAY, DOLL...I'LL TAKE THE CASE. THREE HUNDRED A DAY, PLUS EXPENSES.

IN FACT, I THINK I MAY **ALREADY** HAV⸺ A FEW SUSPECTS...

PIGS IN SPACE!

Starring

CAPTAIN
LINK HOGTHROB

FIRST MATE
MISS PIGGY

And the supercilious
DR STRANGEPORK!

WHEN WE LAST SAW THE GOOD SHIP **SWINETREK**, IT HAD BEEN CHARGED WITH BRINGING A **STRANGE, UNIDENTIFIED SHIP** TO THE INTERGALACTIC AUTHORITIES! **NOW READ ON.**

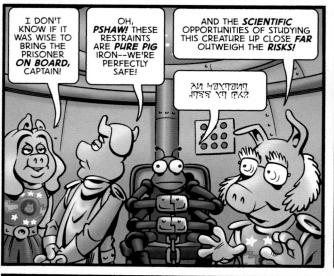

I DON'T KNOW IF IT WAS WISE TO BRING THE PRISONER **ON BOARD,** CAPTAIN!

OH, **PSHAW!** THESE RESTRAINTS ARE **PURE PIG** IRON--WE'RE PERFECTLY SAFE!

AND THE **SCIENTIFIC** OPPORTUNITIES OF STUDYING THIS CREATURE UP CLOSE **FAR** OUTWEIGH THE **RISKS!**

WAIT, WHAT DID HE JUST SAY? STRANGEPORK, YOU SPEAK WEIRDO, WHAT WAS THAT?

I'M TRYING TO NARROW DOWN HIS SPECIES SO I CAN PROGRAM THE **TRANSLATORS!** WITHOUT KNOWING WHERE HE'S FROM, **YOUR** GUESS IS AS GOOD AS **MINE!**

WAIT, WAIT, WAIT. HE WAS **DEFINITELY** LOOKING AT **ME** WHEN HE SAID THAT.

OKAY, THAT MAKES HIM AT LEAST **PART MAMMAL,** THAT NARROWS IT DOWN! KEEP GOING!

LET ME TRY... **HEL-LO SPAACE BUUUG THIIIING! WEEE AAARE FROOOM EEEARRRTHHH!**

WHAT ARE YOU DOING?

I DON'T UNDERSTAND... THAT ALWAYS WORKS IN **SPAIN.**

=SIGH=

RATS! NONE OF THIS MAKES A LICK OF SENSE... RATS, RATS, **RATS!**

YOU CALLED?

OH, HI, RIZZO. SORRY...NO OFFENCE. THIS GONZO BUSINESS IS GETTING ME DOWN.

WHAT GONZO BUSINESS IS THIS? WHEN **HE LANDED ON A POLICEMAN** OR WHEN HE TRIED TO **SET FIRE** TO ONE?

HEH HEH. JANUARY SURE WAS A BAD MONTH TO BE A POLICEMAN, WASN'T IT?

NO, NO, THOSE WERE SETTLED OUT OF COURT. THIS IS ABOUT FIGURING OUT WHAT GONZO ACTUALLY **IS** SO WE CAN **INSURE THE THEATER.**

WHAT HE **IS?** ISN'T **OBVIOUS.**

IS IT?

SURE! HE'S A **GONZO... GONZO THE GREAT!** THE **ONE!** THE **ONLY!** THE **BEST!**

HE'S **UNIQUE,** SCOOTER! **UTTERLY ONE-OF-A KIND!**

YOU KNOW...I GUESS HE **IS!** HE MAY BE A SCRAWNY, HOMELY, UNCATEGORIZABLE **THING**...BUT HE'S **OUR** SCRAWNY, HOMELY, UNCATEGORIZABLE THING!

MISTER SMEDLEY... **YOU'VE GOT YOUR ANSWER!**

ATTABOY! AND I'M **100% BEHIND YA,** AS LONG AS YOU REMEMBER THAT IF IT GOES **WRONG** IT WAS **NOTHING TO DO WITH ME!**

NOW, IF YOU'LL EXCUSE ME, IT'S TIME FOR THE ALL-RODENT MARTIAL ARTS EXTRAVAGANZA THAT IS...

Twinkle Twinkle Little Rat

TWINKLE TWINKLE LITTLE RAT, DO YOU LIKE MY NEW CRAVAT? ALL DRESSED UP TO DO KARATE, JUST IN TIME TO JOIN THE PARTY!

TWINKLE TWINKLE, MIND THAT TEA! PLEASE DON'T POUR IT OVER ME!

TWINKLE, TWINKLE, LITTLE POT, MUST YOU BE SO VERY HOT? FILLED UP WITH THE SWEETEST BREW, WHAT'S AN EARL GREY FIEND TO DO?

TWINKLE, TWINKLE, PUT ME DOWN! LEAVE ME IN MY TEA OF BROWN!

TWINKLE, TWINKLE, NO MORE TEA! THIS WILL BE THE END OF ME! IT'S ALL GONE THE WAY OF DUST. LAUGH AT ME, SIR, IF YOU MUST.

WAIT A MINUTE, MISTER HAT-- LEAVE THIS TO A CLEVER RAT!

TWINKLE, TWINKLE, LITTLE CUP-- HOLD STILL WHILE I FILL YOU UP! COFFEE IS THE WAY TO GO! MADE FROM BEAN GROUNDS, DON'T YOU KNOW?

RIZZO, YOU DESERVE SOME CHEESE! POUR ME TWENTY, IF YOU PLEASE!

MAYBE I WAS SOMEWHAT HASTY-- TWENTY COFFEES AIN'T SO TASTY! TWINKLE, TWINKLE, WHAT A SIGHT! THIS WILL KEEP ME UP ALL NIGHT!

TWINKLE, TWINKLE, WHAT D'YOU THINK?

TWINKLE, TWINKLE--BOY, THEY STINK! HO HO HO!

NICE, GUYS! THEY'LL HAVE TO GET UP EARLY IN THE MORNING TO DO BETTER THAN THAT!

TH-TH-THEY'LL HAVE TO ST-STAY UP ALL N-N-NIGHT!

MISTER SMEDLEY! MISTER SMEDLEY! I'VE FINISHED FILLING OUT THE *FORM* YOU WANTED!

HMM? OH, YES. *EXCELLENT!*

NOW...FROGS, PIGS, CHICKENS, BLAHDY BLAHDY BLAH...AAAND--

Name: GONZO the GREAT

Species: GONZO

criminal record? ☐

conspicuous deformities ☐ YES ☑ NO

OH DEAR.

EVERYTHING A*L*L *RIGHT*, MISTER SMEDLEY?

THAT CREEPY LITTLE GUY...HE WAS *GONZO? GONZO THE GREAT?* GONZO THE *DAREDEVIL KNIFE-JUGGLER, FIRE-EATER, MOTORCYCLE STUNTSTER* GONZO? *THAT* GONZO?

THE ONE! THE ONLY!

OH MY OH MY OH MY...WHERE'S THAT CALCULATOR?...

EVEN *LIVING IN THE SAME TOWN* AS THAT FIEND WILL INCREASE YOUR PREMIUMS! BUT TO BE ACTUALLY *SHARING A THEATER*--! OH ME. OH MY. WE'RE LOOKING AT AN INCREASE OF *AT LEAST* FIVE THOUSAND PER CENT!!

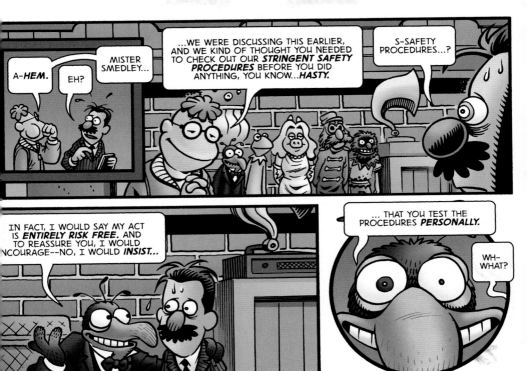

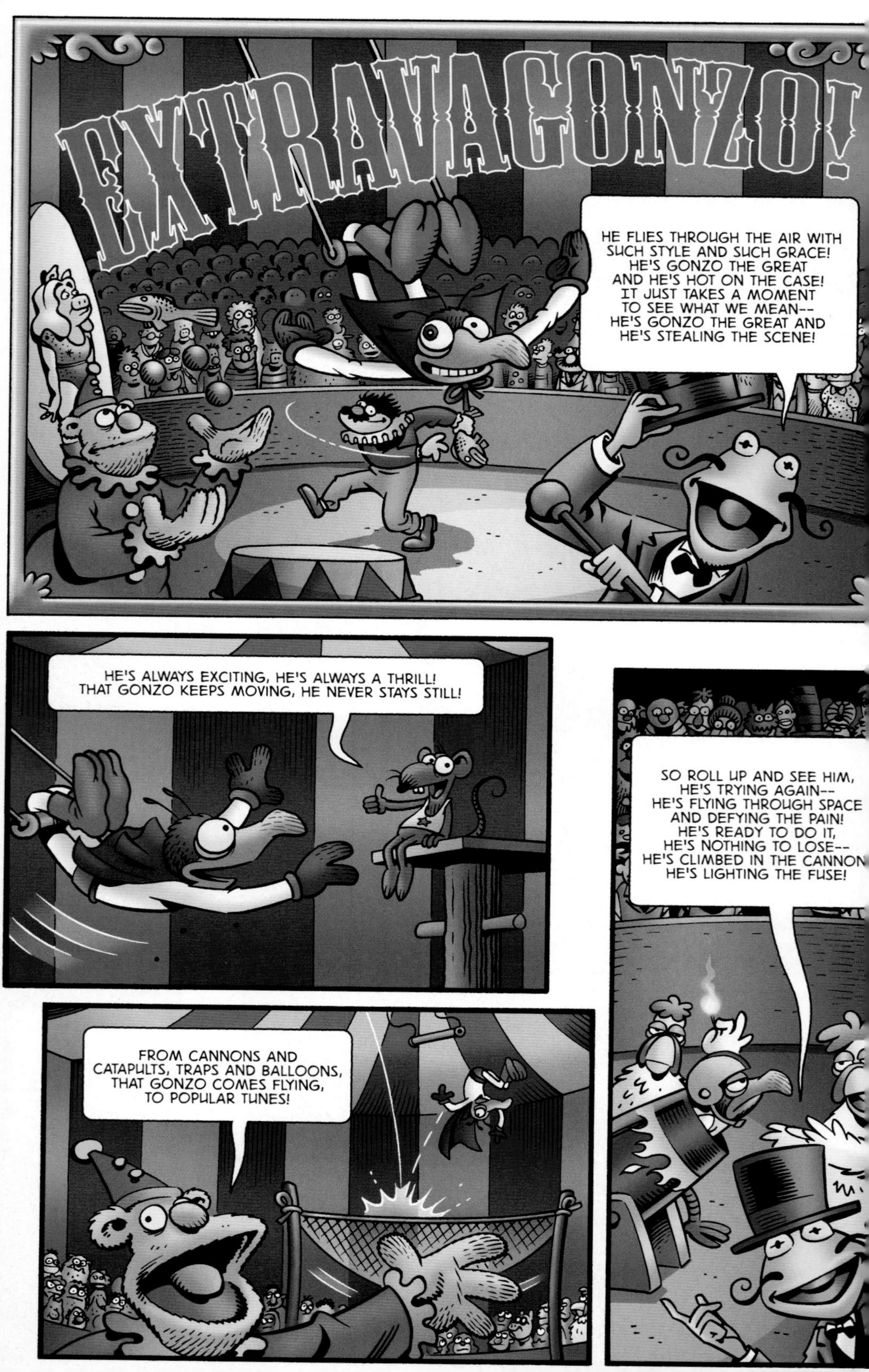
EXTRAVAGONZO!
HE FLIES THROUGH THE AIR WITH SUCH STYLE AND SUCH GRACE! HE'S GONZO THE GREAT AND HE'S HOT ON THE CASE! IT JUST TAKES A MOMENT TO SEE WHAT WE MEAN-- HE'S GONZO THE GREAT AND HE'S STEALING THE SCENE!
HE'S ALWAYS EXCITING, HE'S ALWAYS A THRILL! THAT GONZO KEEPS MOVING, HE NEVER STAYS STILL!
FROM CANNONS AND CATAPULTS, TRAPS AND BALLOONS, THAT GONZO COMES FLYING, TO POPULAR TUNES!
SO ROLL UP AND SEE HIM, HE'S TRYING AGAIN-- HE'S FLYING THROUGH SPACE AND DEFYING THE PAIN! HE'S READY TO DO IT, HE'S NOTHING TO LOSE-- HE'S CLIMBED IN THE CANNON HE'S LIGHTING THE FUSE!

HE'S GONZO THE GREAT, AND HOW GREATLY HE FELL.
HIS COLLARBONE'S BROKEN, HE'S NOT VERY WELL.
THEY SAY HE'LL BE HERE TILL NEXT THURSDAY, AT LEAST--
HE'S GONZO THE GREATEST...

...THE MYSTERY BEAST.

WE'LL COME BY AGAIN TOMORROW, GONZO. DON'T WORRY--THEY'LL HAVE YOU UP AND ABOUT IN NO TIME!

THEY ALWAYS *DO,* DON'T THEY?

THANKS FOR COMING, SCOOTER. I'M SORRY I WON'T BE PERFORMING FOR A WHILE.

DON'T WORRY ABOUT GONZO

GONZO...I NEED TO ASK YOU SOMETHING. IT'S DRIVING ME NUTS. I JUST *HAVE* TO KNOW.

TELL ME...PLEASE...*WHAT THE HECK ARE YOU??*

OH, SCOOTER...I THOUGHT YOU KNEW.

I'M AN *ARTIST.*

AN ARTIST.

WELL...I GUESS HE *IS,* AFTER ALL.

The End

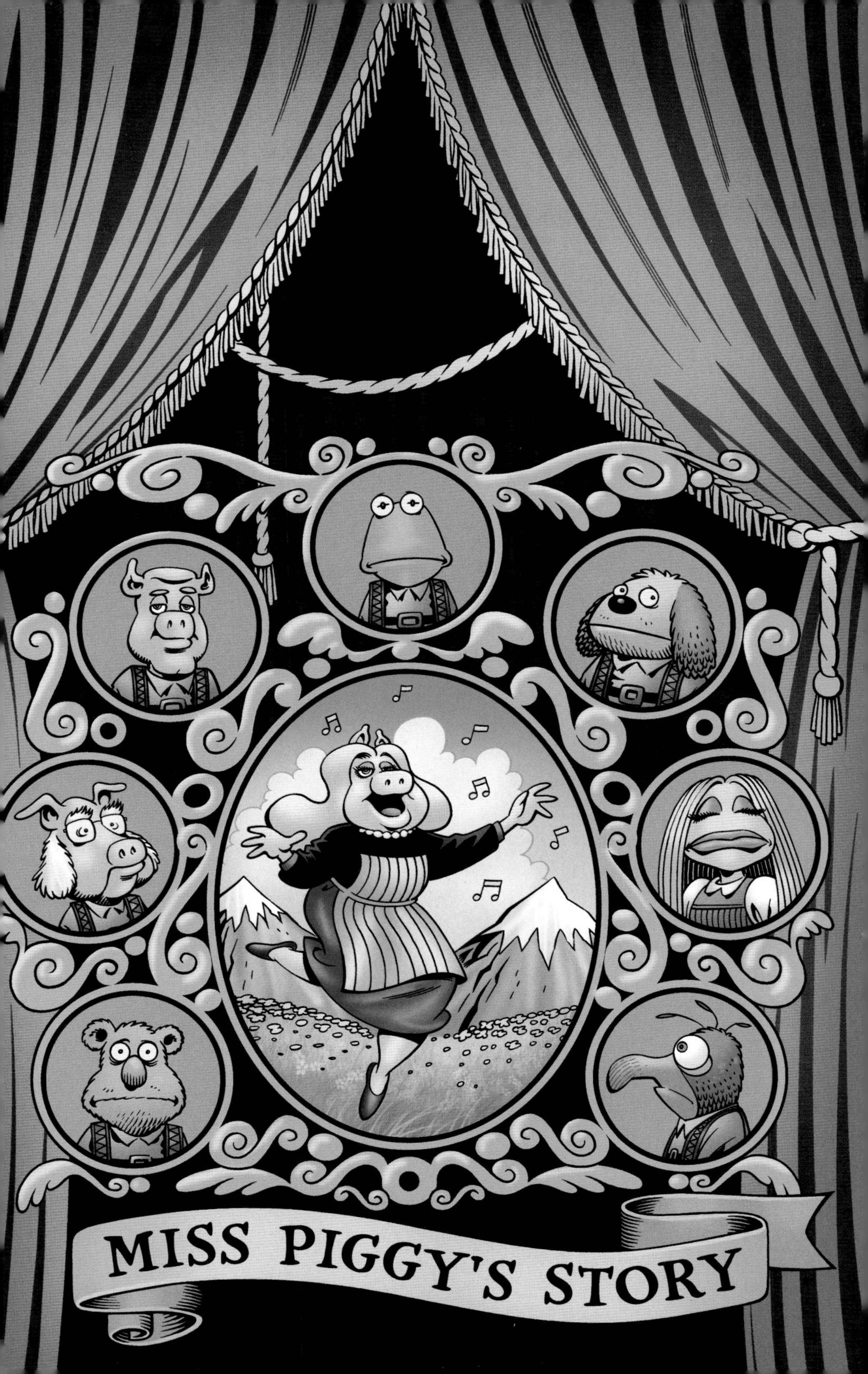
MISS PIGGY'S STORY

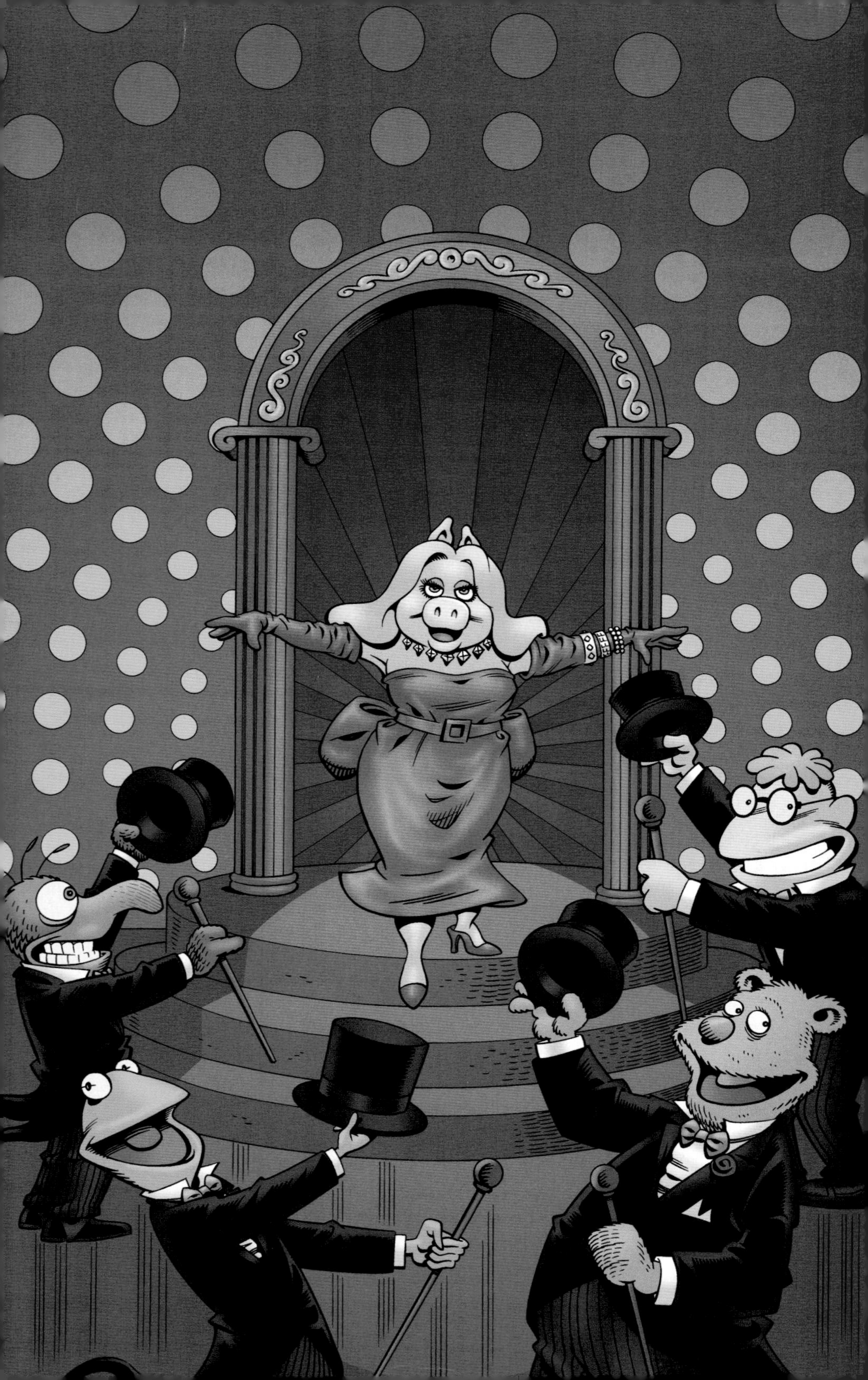

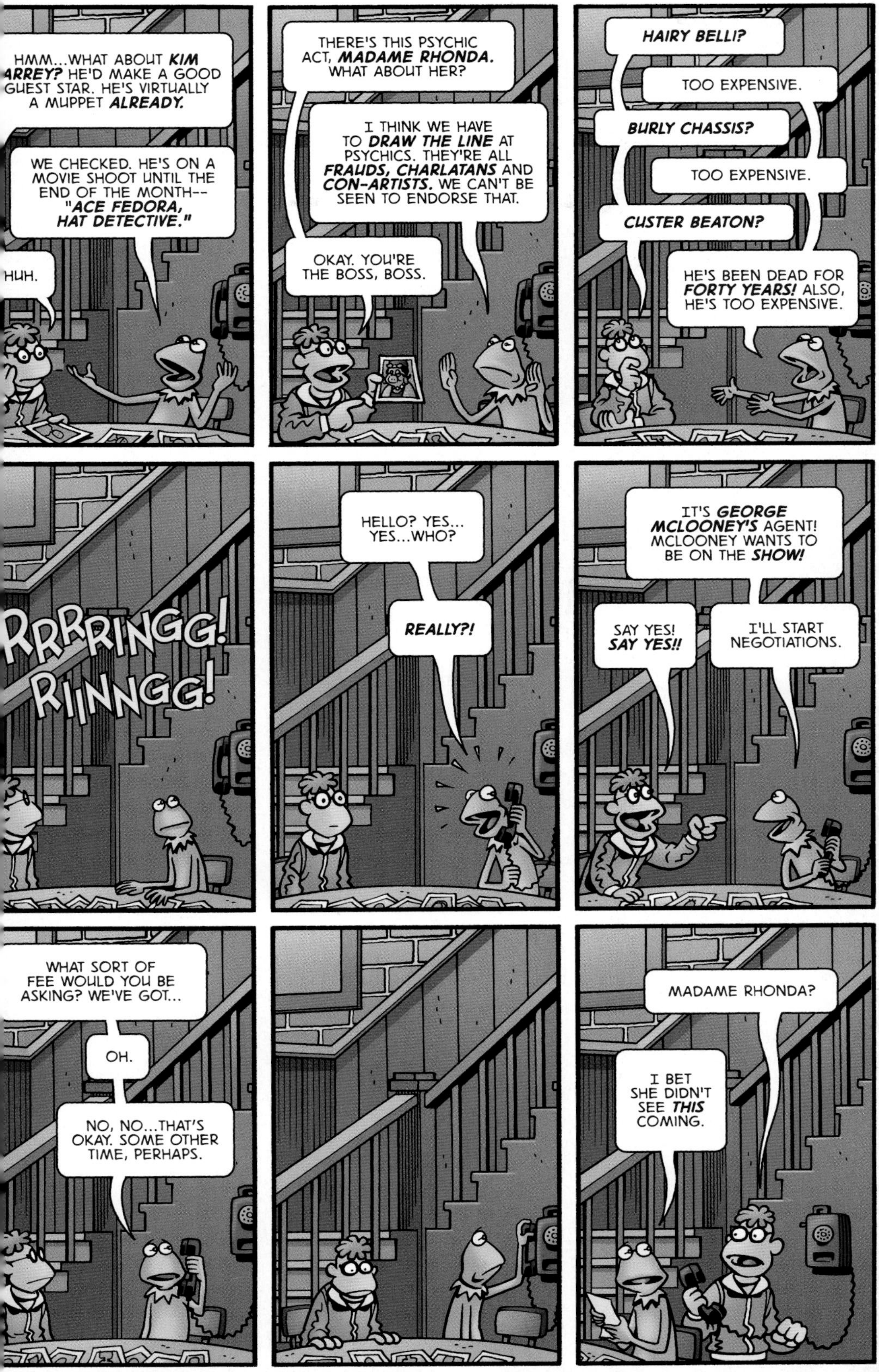
HMM...WHAT ABOUT KIM ARREY? HE'D MAKE A GOOD GUEST STAR. HE'S VIRTUALLY A MUPPET ALREADY.
WE CHECKED. HE'S ON A MOVIE SHOOT UNTIL THE END OF THE MONTH-- "ACE FEDORA, HAT DETECTIVE."
HUH.
THERE'S THIS PSYCHIC ACT, MADAME RHONDA. WHAT ABOUT HER?
I THINK WE HAVE TO DRAW THE LINE AT PSYCHICS. THEY'RE ALL FRAUDS, CHARLATANS AND CON-ARTISTS. WE CAN'T BE SEEN TO ENDORSE THAT.
OKAY. YOU'RE THE BOSS, BOSS.
HAIRY BELLI?
TOO EXPENSIVE.
BURLY CHASSIS?
TOO EXPENSIVE.
CUSTER BEATON?
HE'S BEEN DEAD FOR FORTY YEARS! ALSO, HE'S TOO EXPENSIVE.
RRRRINGG! RIINNGG!
HELLO? YES... YES...WHO?
REALLY?!
IT'S GEORGE MCLOONEY'S AGENT! MCLOONEY WANTS TO BE ON THE SHOW!
SAY YES! SAY YES!!
I'LL START NEGOTIATIONS.
WHAT SORT OF FEE WOULD YOU BE ASKING? WE'VE GOT...
OH.
NO, NO...THAT'S OKAY. SOME OTHER TIME, PERHAPS.
MADAME RHONDA?
I BET SHE DIDN'T SEE THIS COMING.

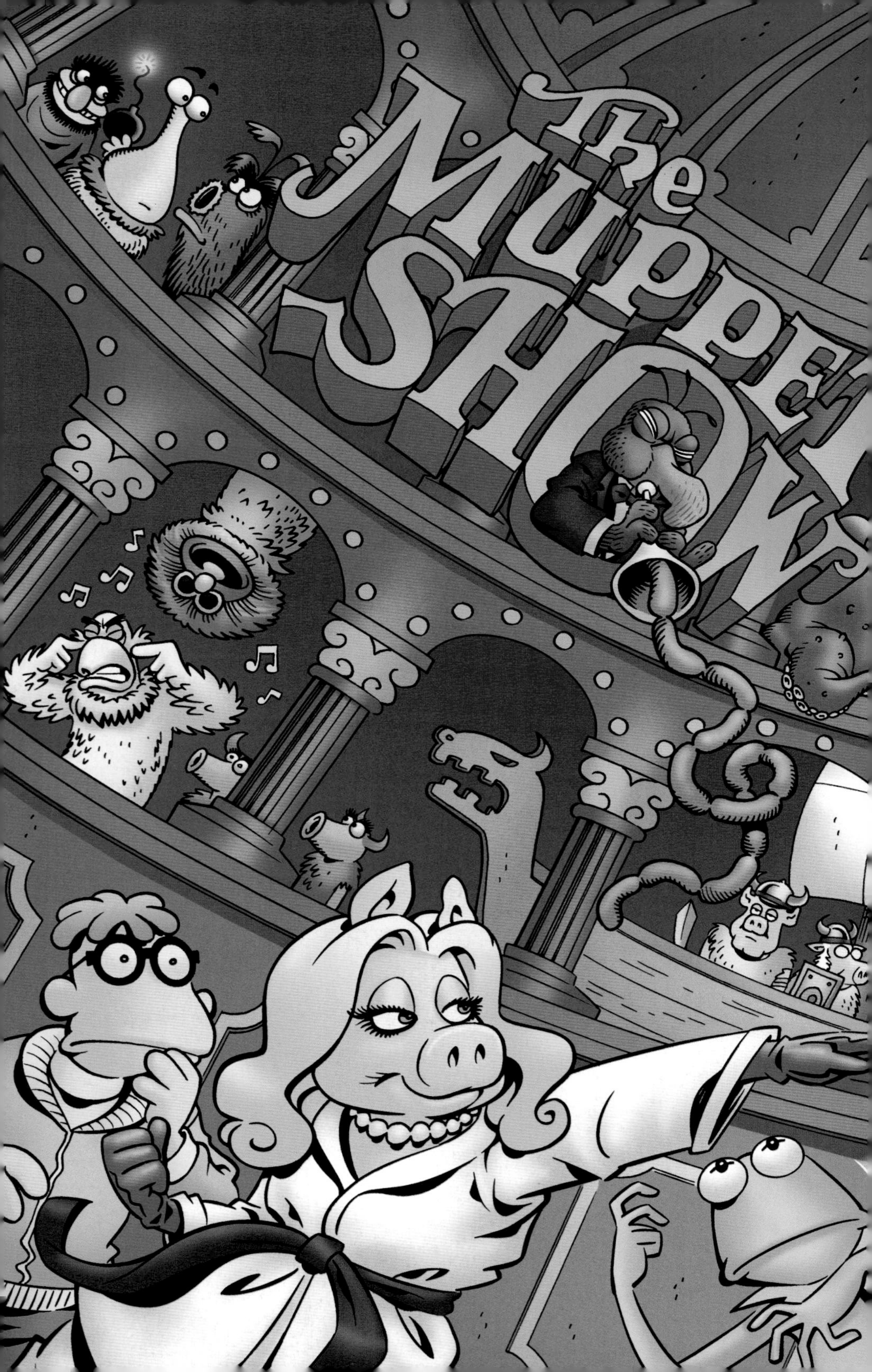

The Muppet Show

MADAME RHONDA? WHO THE HECK IS MADAME RHONDA?

OH, I THINK I'VE HEARD OF HER. SHE'S A MYSTIC.

A *MISTAKE?*

NO, THAT WAS WHAT WE MADE WHEN WE *CAME* HERE! *HO HO HO!*

HERE, GIVE ME YOUR PALM. I USED TO READ THEM MYSELF--IT'S *AMAZING* WHAT YOU PICK UP IN THE ARMY!

OKAY. CAN YOU SEE ANYTHING?

HMMM...

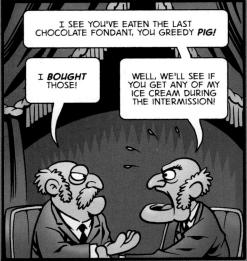

I SEE YOU'VE EATEN THE LAST CHOCOLATE FONDANT, YOU GREEDY *PIG!*

I *BOUGHT* THOSE!

WELL, WE'LL SEE IF YOU GET ANY OF MY ICE CREAM DURING THE INTERMISSION!

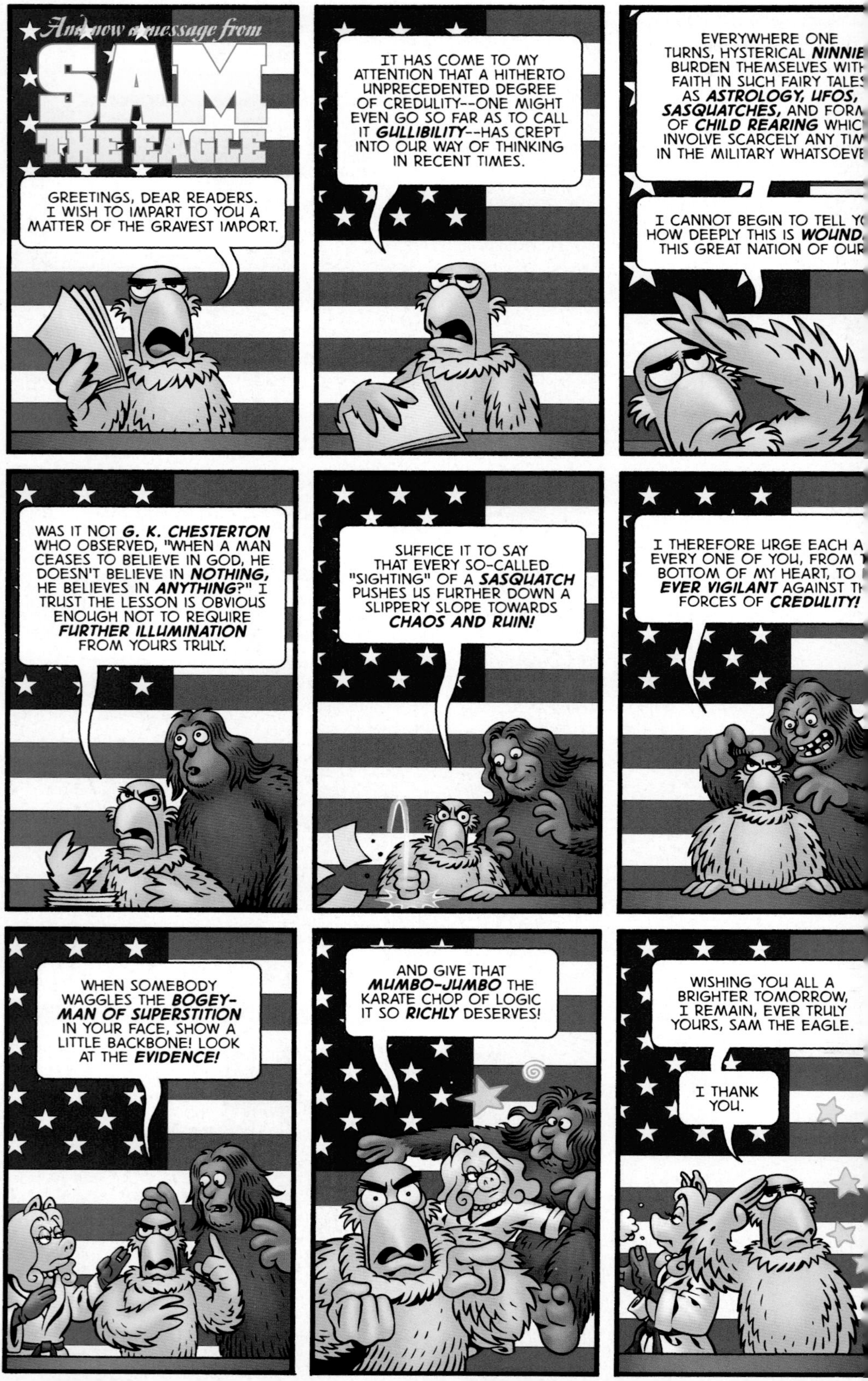
And now a message from
SAM THE EAGLE
GREETINGS, DEAR READERS. I WISH TO IMPART TO YOU A MATTER OF THE GRAVEST IMPORT.
IT HAS COME TO MY ATTENTION THAT A HITHERTO UNPRECEDENTED DEGREE OF CREDULITY--ONE MIGHT EVEN GO SO FAR AS TO CALL IT GULLIBILITY--HAS CREPT INTO OUR WAY OF THINKING IN RECENT TIMES.
EVERYWHERE ONE TURNS, HYSTERICAL NINNIE BURDEN THEMSELVES WITH FAITH IN SUCH FAIRY TALES AS ASTROLOGY, UFOS, SASQUATCHES, AND FORM OF CHILD REARING WHIC INVOLVE SCARCELY ANY TIM IN THE MILITARY WHATSOEVE
I CANNOT BEGIN TO TELL YO HOW DEEPLY THIS IS WOUND THIS GREAT NATION OF OUR
WAS IT NOT G. K. CHESTERTON WHO OBSERVED, "WHEN A MAN CEASES TO BELIEVE IN GOD, HE DOESN'T BELIEVE IN NOTHING, HE BELIEVES IN ANYTHING?" I TRUST THE LESSON IS OBVIOUS ENOUGH NOT TO REQUIRE FURTHER ILLUMINATION FROM YOURS TRULY.
SUFFICE IT TO SAY THAT EVERY SO-CALLED "SIGHTING" OF A SASQUATCH PUSHES US FURTHER DOWN A SLIPPERY SLOPE TOWARDS CHAOS AND RUIN!
I THEREFORE URGE EACH A EVERY ONE OF YOU, FROM T BOTTOM OF MY HEART, TO EVER VIGILANT AGAINST TH FORCES OF CREDULITY!
WHEN SOMEBODY WAGGLES THE BOGEY-MAN OF SUPERSTITION IN YOUR FACE, SHOW A LITTLE BACKBONE! LOOK AT THE EVIDENCE!
AND GIVE THAT MUMBO-JUMBO THE KARATE CHOP OF LOGIC IT SO RICHLY DESERVES!
WISHING YOU ALL A BRIGHTER TOMORROW, I REMAIN, EVER TRULY YOURS, SAM THE EAGLE.
I THANK YOU.

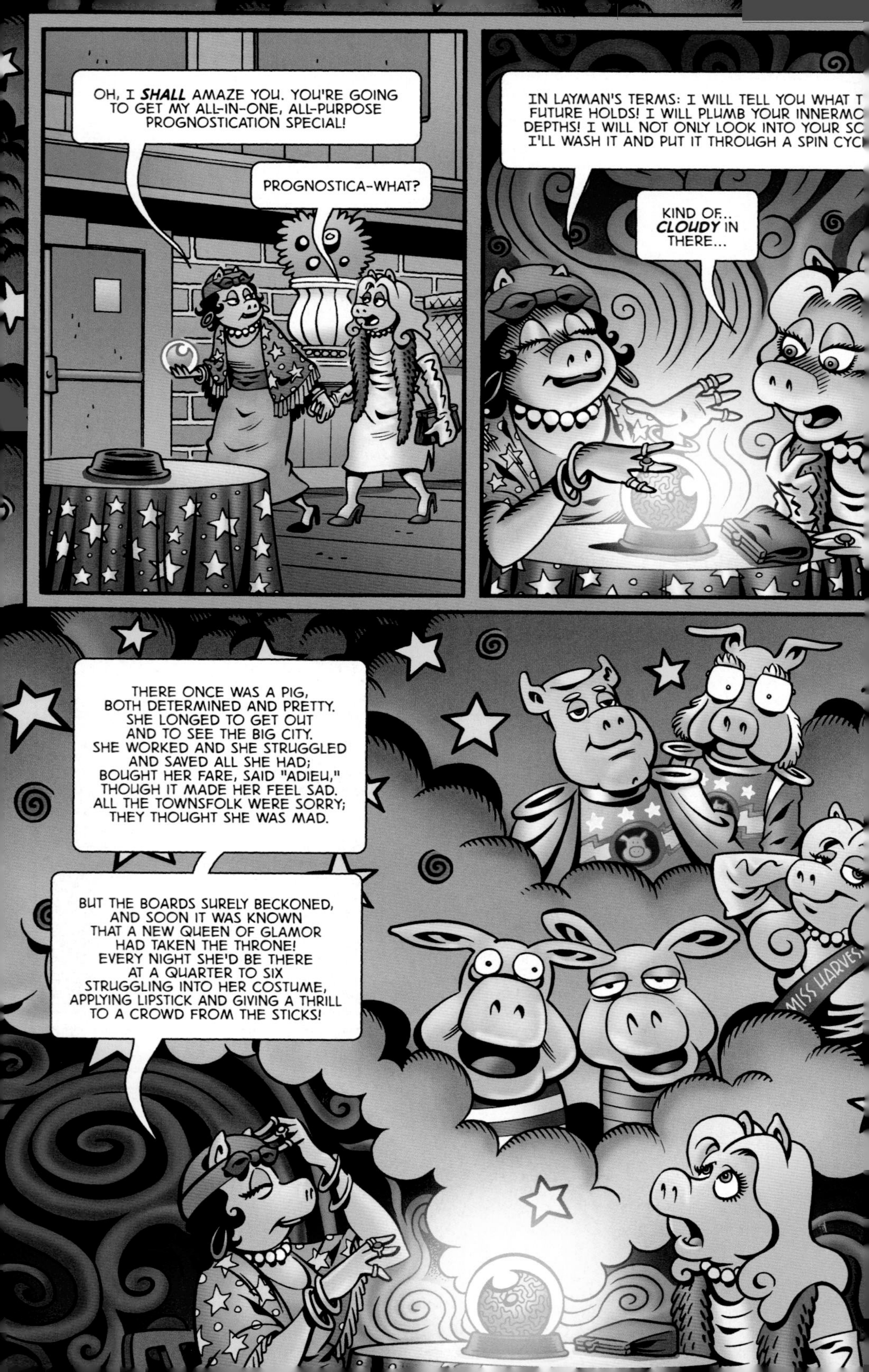
OH, I *SHALL* AMAZE YOU. YOU'RE GOING TO GET MY ALL-IN-ONE, ALL-PURPOSE PROGNOSTICATION SPECIAL!
PROGNOSTICA-WHAT?
IN LAYMAN'S TERMS: I WILL TELL YOU WHAT T FUTURE HOLDS! I WILL PLUMB YOUR INNERMO DEPTHS! I WILL NOT ONLY LOOK INTO YOUR SO I'LL WASH IT AND PUT IT THROUGH A SPIN CYC
KIND OF... *CLOUDY* IN THERE...
THERE ONCE WAS A PIG, BOTH DETERMINED AND PRETTY. SHE LONGED TO GET OUT AND TO SEE THE BIG CITY. SHE WORKED AND SHE STRUGGLED AND SAVED ALL SHE HAD; BOUGHT HER FARE, SAID "ADIEU," THOUGH IT MADE HER FEEL SAD. ALL THE TOWNSFOLK WERE SORRY; THEY THOUGHT SHE WAS MAD.
BUT THE BOARDS SURELY BECKONED, AND SOON IT WAS KNOWN THAT A NEW QUEEN OF GLAMOR HAD TAKEN THE THRONE! EVERY NIGHT SHE'D BE THERE AT A QUARTER TO SIX STRUGGLING INTO HER COSTUME, APPLYING LIPSTICK AND GIVING A THRILL TO A CROWD FROM THE STICKS!
MISS HARVES

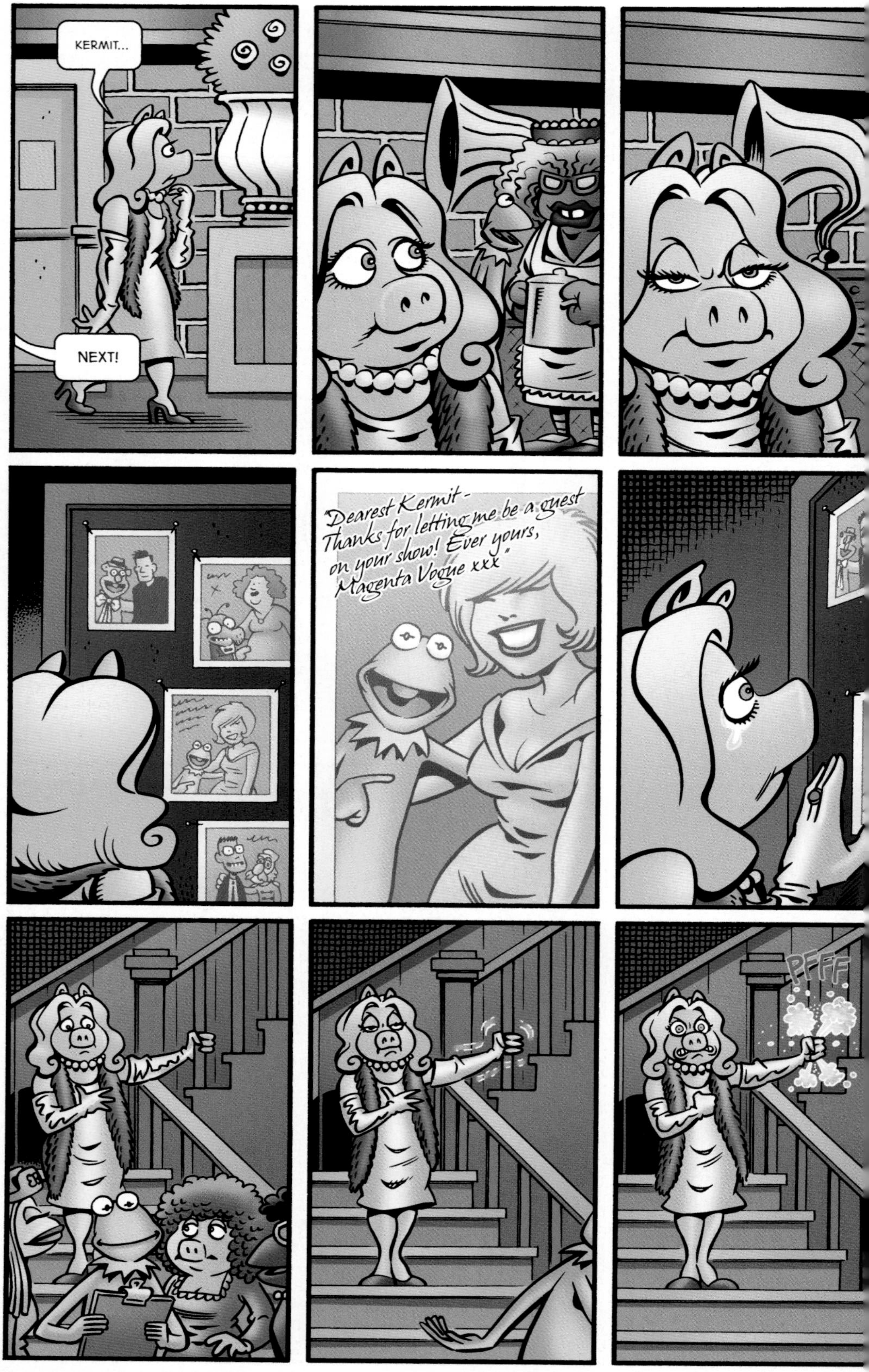
KERMIT...
NEXT!
"Dearest Kermit - Thanks for letting me be a guest on your show! Ever yours, Magenta Vogue xxx"
PFFF

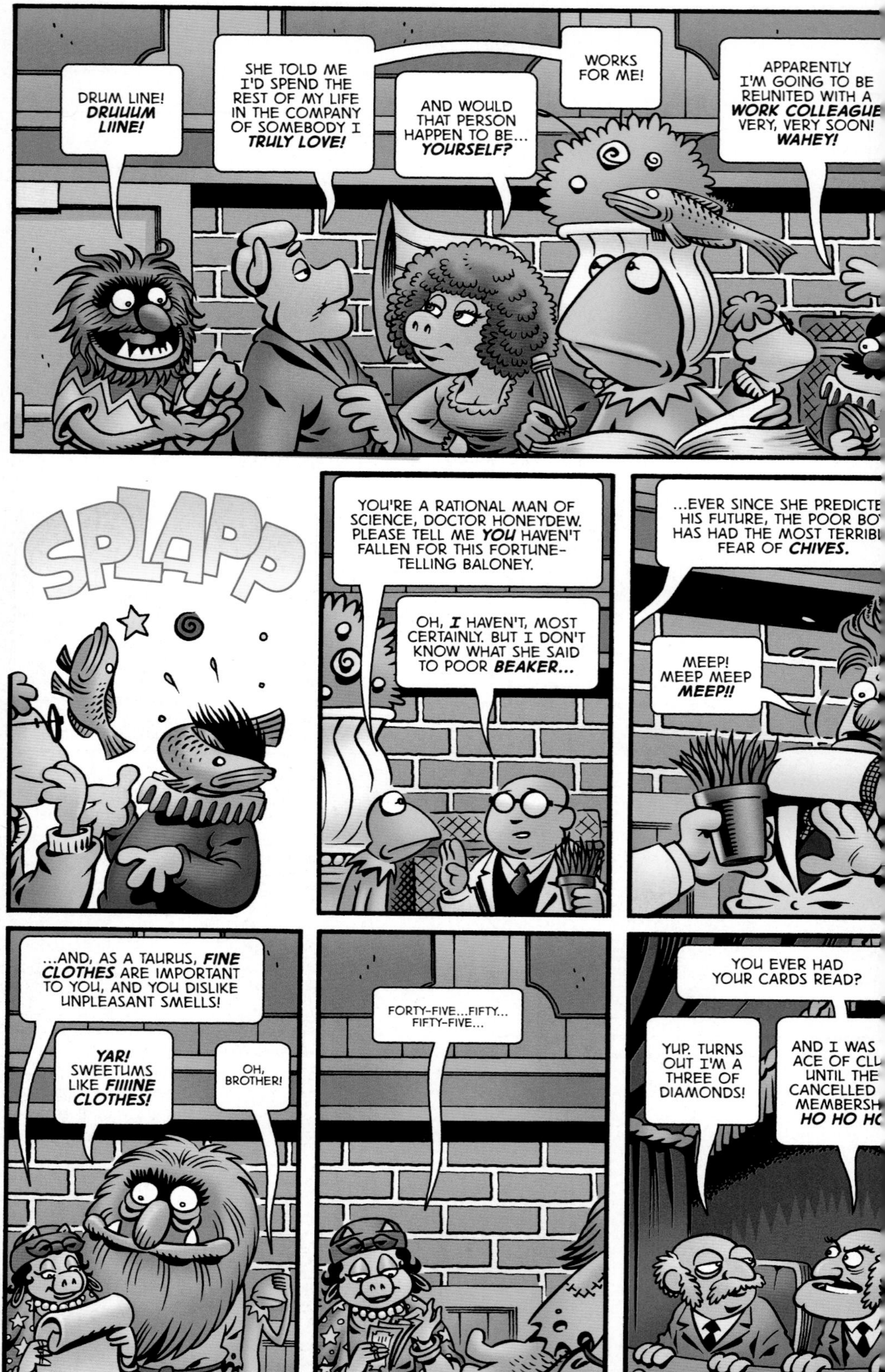
DRUM LINE! DRUUUM LIINE!
SHE TOLD ME I'D SPEND THE REST OF MY LIFE IN THE COMPANY OF SOMEBODY I TRULY LOVE!
AND WOULD THAT PERSON HAPPEN TO BE... YOURSELF?
WORKS FOR ME!
APPARENTLY I'M GOING TO BE REUNITED WITH A WORK COLLEAGUE VERY, VERY SOON! WAHEY!
SPLAPP
YOU'RE A RATIONAL MAN OF SCIENCE, DOCTOR HONEYDEW. PLEASE TELL ME YOU HAVEN'T FALLEN FOR THIS FORTUNE-TELLING BALONEY.
OH, I HAVEN'T, MOST CERTAINLY. BUT I DON'T KNOW WHAT SHE SAID TO POOR BEAKER...
...EVER SINCE SHE PREDICTE HIS FUTURE, THE POOR BO HAS HAD THE MOST TERRIBL FEAR OF CHIVES.
MEEP! MEEP MEEP MEEP!!
...AND, AS A TAURUS, FINE CLOTHES ARE IMPORTANT TO YOU, AND YOU DISLIKE UNPLEASANT SMELLS!
YAR! SWEETUMS LIKE FIIIINE CLOTHES!
OH, BROTHER!
FORTY-FIVE...FIFTY... FIFTY-FIVE...
YOU EVER HAD YOUR CARDS READ?
YUP. TURNS OUT I'M A THREE OF DIAMONDS!
AND I WAS ACE OF CL UNTIL THE CANCELLED MEMBERSH HO HO H

LET'S LISTEN IN ON THE...
TALKING HOUSES
I THINK IT'S "FOR SALE, NO REASONABLE OFFER REFUSED".
I WAS TOLD I'D MEET A HANDSOME NEW NEIGHBOR-- BUT IT TURNED OUT I COULDN'T IGNORE HIS BAY WINDOW!
OH, THAT'S TOO BAD. WHEN I SAW HIS CHIMNEY POT, I WAS SURE SPARKS WERE GOING TO FLY!
IT WOULD NEVER HAVE LASTED, ANYWAY--NOT SOMETHING BUILT ON SUCH WEAK FOUNDATIONS!
DID YOU HEAR ABOUT THAT GUY WHO HAD HIS PALM READ?
THAT'S NOTHING-- I HAD MY BRICKS RED!
HAVE YOU EVER HELD A CRYSTAL BALL?
NO, BUT I'M PRETTY SURE I'VE HELD A TUPPERWARE PARTY...
IS THIS SKIT NEARLY OVER? MY PYLONS ARE KILLING ME!

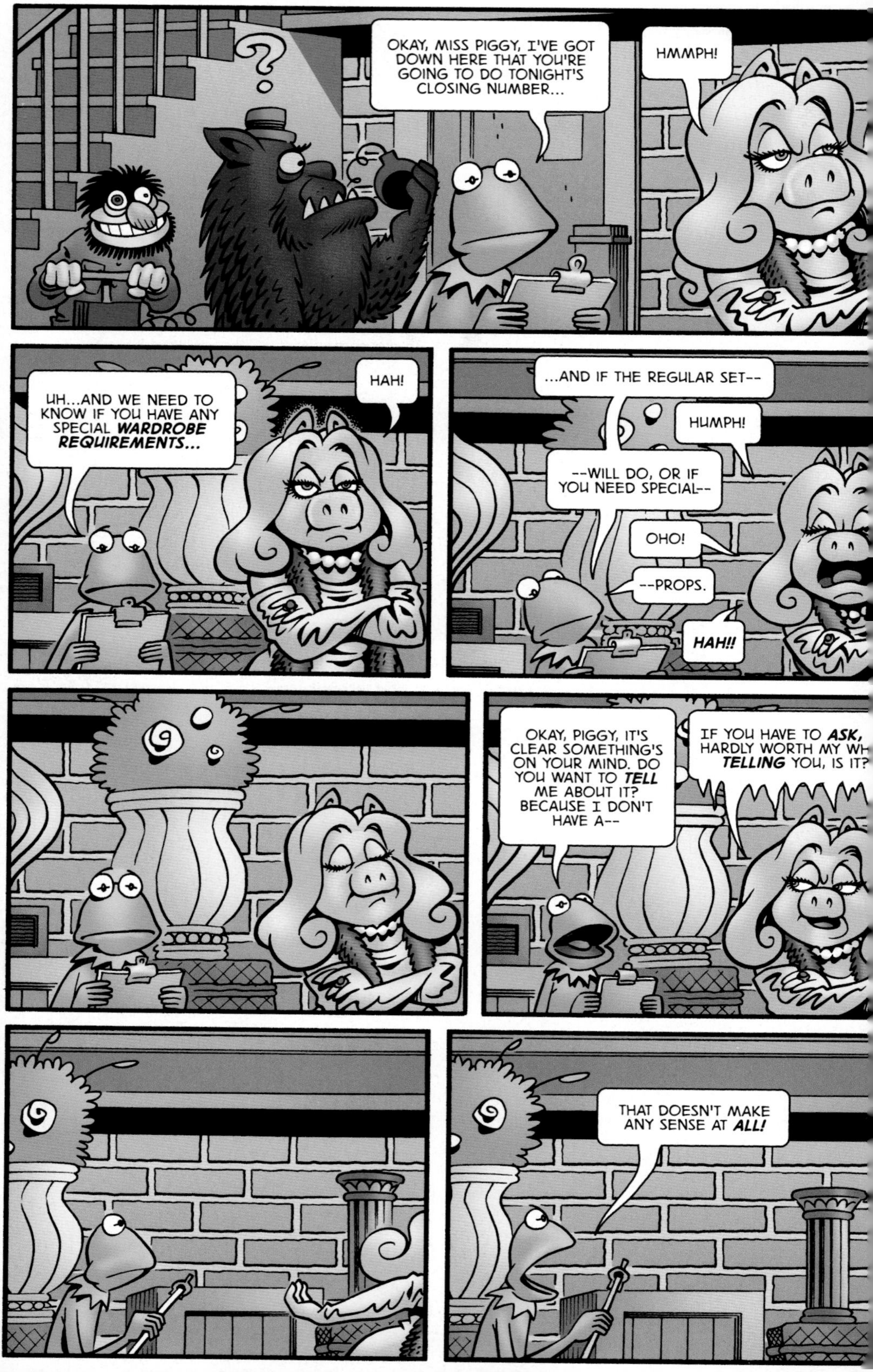
OKAY, MISS PIGGY, I'VE GOT DOWN HERE THAT YOU'RE GOING TO DO TONIGHT'S CLOSING NUMBER...
HMMPH!
UH...AND WE NEED TO KNOW IF YOU HAVE ANY SPECIAL ***WARDROBE REQUIREMENTS...***
HAH!
...AND IF THE REGULAR SET--
HUMPH!
--WILL DO, OR IF YOU NEED SPECIAL--
OHO!
--PROPS.
HAH!!
OKAY, PIGGY, IT'S CLEAR SOMETHING'S ON YOUR MIND. DO YOU WANT TO ***TELL*** ME ABOUT IT? BECAUSE I DON'T HAVE A--
IF YOU HAVE TO ***ASK,*** HARDLY WORTH MY WH ***TELLING*** YOU, IS IT?
THAT DOESN'T MAKE ANY SENSE AT ***ALL!***

AND NOW, OVER TO...

MUPPET LABS

WHERE THE **FUTURE** IS BEING **MADE** TODAY!

GREETINGS! I AM *DOCTOR BUNSEN HONEYDEW,* AND THIS IS MY ASSISTANT, *BEAKER!* SAY HELLO, BEAKER.

MEEP.

THANK YOU, BEAKER. TODAY I WILL DEMONSTRATE HOW THAT WHICH APPEARS TO BE "PSYCHIC ABILITY" EXISTS IN *ALL* OF US TO SOME SMALL DEGREE--ACTUALLY A COMBINATION OF *INTUITION, COMMON SENSE* AND *SHEER GOOD FORTUNE!*

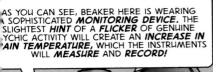

AS YOU CAN SEE, BEAKER HERE IS WEARING A SOPHISTICATED *MONITORING DEVICE.* THE SLIGHTEST *HINT* OF A *FLICKER* OF GENUINE PSYCHIC ACTIVITY WILL CREATE AN *INCREASE IN BRAIN TEMPERATURE,* WHICH THE INSTRUMENTS WILL *MEASURE* AND *RECORD!*

MEEP MEEP MEEP?

OH, *YES,* BEAKER--THE INCREASE WILL BE SO *SLIGHT,* IT WILL BE IMPERCEPTIBLE TO ALL BUT THE MOST *DELICATE* SCIENTIFIC INSTRUMENTS!

MEEP.

YOU'RE WELCOME. AND I'M GLAD YOUR MOTHER IS GETTING BETTER.

NOW, BEAKER-- WOULD YOU MAKE SO BOLD AS TO HAZARD A GUESS AT WHICH CARD I'M HOLDING?

MMMM... M-MEEP?

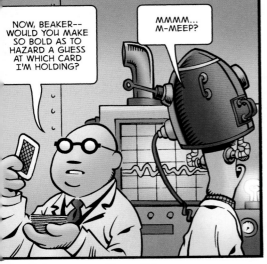

HMM...*UNCANNY.* BEGINNER'S LUCK, NO DOUBT.

ALL RIGHT, BEAKER, LET'S TRY SOMETHING A LITTLE MORE CHALLENGING! WHICH TWO CARDS AM I HOLDING UP?
MM-M-MEEEEEP...? MEEP.
GOOD HEAVENS, BEAKER! THIS IS REALLY QUITE ASTONISHING! YOU'RE GETTING A PERFECT RECORD HERE!
THE NEXT TEST MUST BE MORE CHALLENGING STILL--AND I THINK I KNOW JUST THE THING!
NOW...UURGH!...WHAT...WHAT AM I HOLDING UP...OOF!...NOW...?
EEURGH!
MMMMMM... MEEP MEEP?
FOOF
OH, BEAKER, YOU'VE GONE ON FIRE. PLEASE DON'T GO ON FIRE.
MUH-MUH-MEEEEE MEEP MEEP MEEEEP!!! MEEEEEP!!
TERRIBLE! HEY, GUESS WHO I HAD LUNCH WITH TODAY?
OH, I DUNNO... OSCAR MAYER?
FOOF

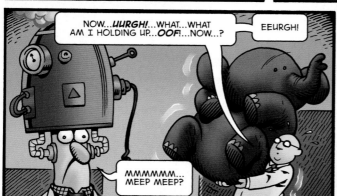

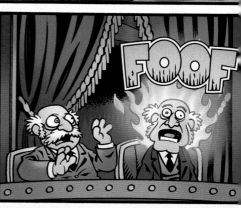

...AND THAT MAKES *YOU*, KERMIT OL' PAL, THE *LAST* OF US NOT TO HAVE HIS FORTUNE TOLD!

FOR GOOD REASON. PSYCHICS ARE FULL OF *HOOEY.*

OH, BUT I DON'T THINK THAT *IS* THE REASON! I THINK YOU'RE JUST... *CHICKEN.*

BUK BUK

MADAME RHONDA

FORTUNES TOLD! INQUIRE WITHIN

BUK BUK BAAARK

BUURK BUK BUK BUK

BUUUUK BUK BUK BUK BUK

KNOCK IT OFF. THIS IS *CHILDISH* AND *RIDICULOUS* AND I'M NOT HAVING ANYTHING TO DO WITH IT.

HEY, MISTER KERMIT! HAVE YOU HAD YOUR FORTUNE TOLD YET?

NOT *YOU TOO,* BEAUREGARD!

OH YEAH! I'M REALLY GOING TO *CLEAN UP* IN THE NEAR FUTURE!

I SEE WHAT YOU DID THERE! *CLEVER!*

BUK BUK BUK BGARK!

LL YOU T THAT OUT?!

OH.

COME ON NOW, KERMIT. HUMOR US.

YEAH. WHAT'S THE WORST THAT COULD HAPPEN?

ALL RIGHT! IF IT'LL STOP THIS *SCHOOLYARD BULLYING,* I'LL DO IT. AND I GUARANTEE IT'LL BE *HORSE FEATHERS* FROM *START TO FINISH!*

AD

MA

And now it's time for...

PIGS IN SPACE!

Starring

CAPTAIN LINK HOGTHROB

FIRST MATE MISS PIGGY

And the propinquitous DR STRANGEPORK!

WHEN WE LAST LEFT THE SHIP *SWINETREK*, THEY HAD JUST BEEN *DEFLECTED* FROM THEIR PROGRAMMED COURSE BY A *SURPRISE METEOR SHOWER*--AND FORCED TO STEER INTO *UNMAPPED TERRITORY!*

NOW READ ON...

THESE READINGS, LINK--THEY'RE *OFF THE SCALE!* THE *BACKGROUND PSYCHIC ENERGY* IS *COLOSSAL!*

MEANING WHAT, EXACTLY?

WHY, FIRST MATE PIGGY, *EVERYONE* KNOWS WHAT THAT MEANS! DON'T YOU RECALL THE SORRY FATE OF THE *USS PORKCHOP?*

YOU DON'T MEAN--

YES! FOR AS LONG AS WE STAY HERE..

...WE'LL BE ABLE TO *READ ONE ANOTHER'S MINDS!*

HUH. WELL, THAT DOESN'T SOUND SO BAD. UNLESS YOU'VE GOT SOMETHING TO *HIDE...*

IT'S NOT THAT SIMPLE, PIGGY. A PHENOMENON SUCH AS THIS CAN STRIP AWAY THE VENEER OF CIVILIZED BEHAVIOR THAT ENABLES US TO FUNCTION AS A COMMUNITY!

EN ANGLAIS, S'IL VOUS PLAÎT...

WHEN YOU TALK TO ME, I'LL BE ABLE TO KNOW WHAT YOU'RE *REALLY* THINKING.

OH.

STOP TRYING TO FRIGHTE ME, YOU MUTTONCHOP-WHISKERED BABOON.

AT? **WHAT?** WHAT HAPPENED THERE?

M AFRAID STARTING LREADY. **MUTTON-CHOP-- HISKERED ABOON"**, AM I?

BUT I DIDN'T SAY--

YOU DON'T **HAVE** TO SAY IT! THAT'S WHAT I'VE BEEN TRYING TO **TELL YOU!**

TEN YEARS OF TRAINING AND I END UP BEING ASSIGNED TO **THESE** CHOWDERHEADS!

I KNOW WHAT'S HAPPENING HERE AND I WILL OVERLOOK ANY UNFLATTERING REMARKS FOR THE GOOD OF THE MISSION.

I WILL BREAK EVERY BONE IN YOUR SCRAWNY GIRLISH BODY WHEN ALL THIS IS OVER.

NOW, LET'S KEEP THINGS **PROFESSIONAL!** WE'RE SIMPLY GOING TO HAVE TO **IGNORE** THOSE LITTLE VOICES IN OUR HEADS AND MAKE THE **BEST** OF THINGS UNTIL WE'RE CLEAR OF THE **PSYCHIC ENERGY ZONE!** OKAY?

I AM A BEAUTIFUL, HANDSOME MAN, EVERYBODY LOVES ME AND I WANT MY MOMMY.

THANKS, LINK! E NEEDED YOUR ICE OF REASON KEEP THINGS IN PERSPECTIVE!

I HAVE ALWAYS OUGHT YOU WERE OMPOUS TWIT AND R LAST SPEECH HAS ONE NOTHING TO HANGE MY MIND.

WHY, **THANK YOU,** DOCTOR.

HEY, **BOYS...**

I AM A BEAUTIFUL, HANDSOME MAN, EVERYBODY LOVES ME AND I WANT MY MOMMY.

...AM I IMAGINING THINGS, OR IS THAT SHIP APPROACHING US THE INFAMOUS **SPACE PIRATE, SHIVERS MCTIMBERS?**

I KNOW **EXACTLY** WHAT IT IS, BUT I HAVE TO PHRASE IT AS A QUESTION SO YOU ROCKET JOCKEYS THINK YOU'RE HAVING ALL THE BRIGHT IDEAS YOURSELVES.

OH MY.

THROW THEM MISS Y, I MIGHT YET SAVE MY OWN SKIN!

OH MY.

I WANT MY MOMMY.

OH, BROTHER.

OH, BROTHER.

WILL FIRST MATE PIGGY BE THROWN TO THE PIRATES?

HAS DOCTOR STRANGEPORK GOT REALLY FIRST-RATE HEALTH CARE?

DOES LINK HOGTHROB REALLY WANT HIS MOMMY OR WILL ANYBODY'S MOMMY DO JUST AS WELL? TUNE IN NEXT WEEK TO THE SUB-ETHER WAVE NETWORK AND CATCH AN EXTRA-DIMENSIONAL REMAKE OF...

PIGS IN SPAAACE!

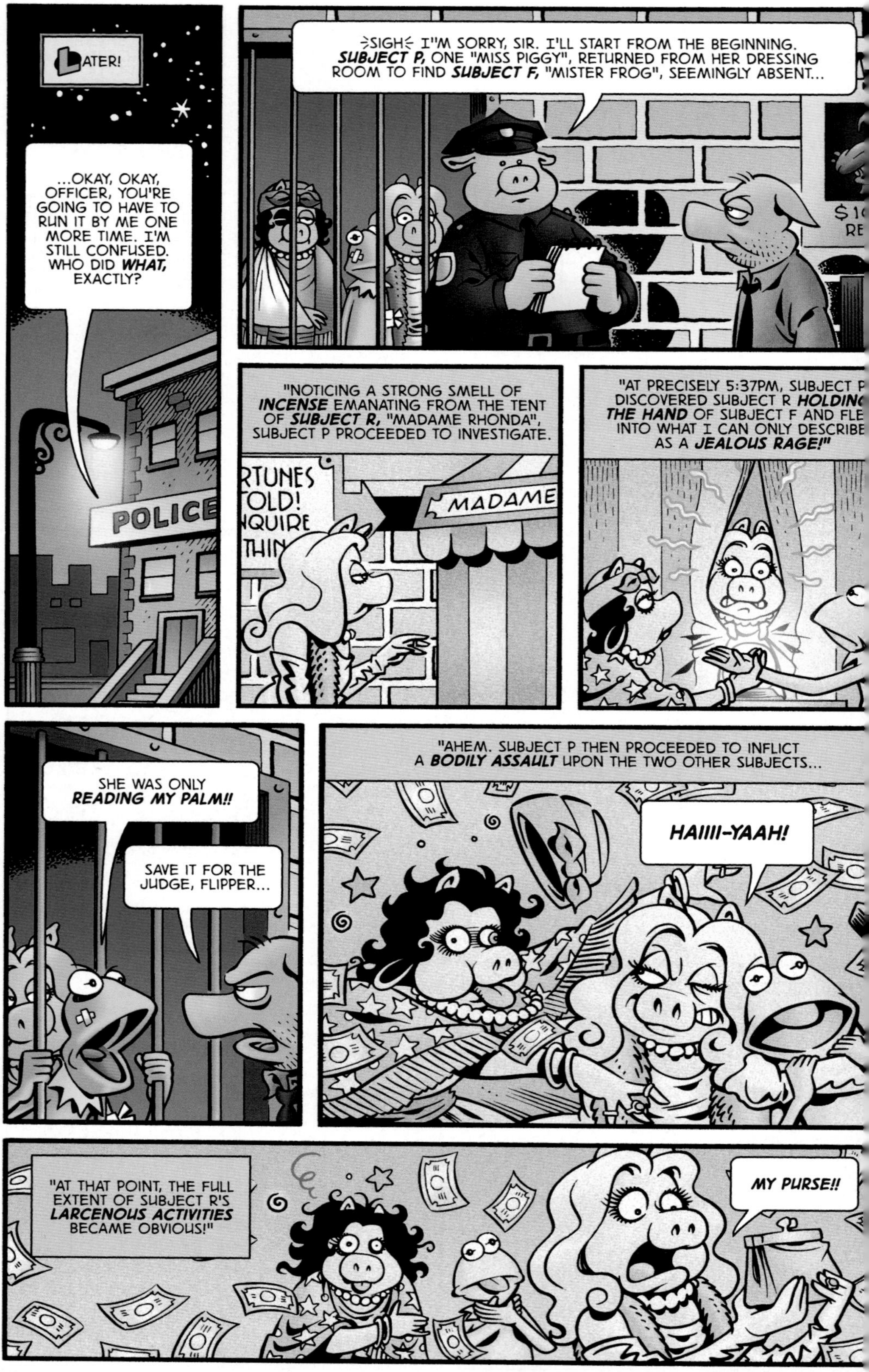
LATER!
...OKAY, OKAY, OFFICER, YOU'RE GOING TO HAVE TO RUN IT BY ME ONE MORE TIME. I'M STILL CONFUSED. WHO DID *WHAT,* EXACTLY?
POLICE
⇒SIGH⇐ I'M SORRY, SIR. I'LL START FROM THE BEGINNING. ***SUBJECT P,*** ONE "MISS PIGGY", RETURNED FROM HER DRESSING ROOM TO FIND ***SUBJECT F,*** "MISTER FROG", SEEMINGLY ABSENT...
"NOTICING A STRONG SMELL OF ***INCENSE*** EMANATING FROM THE TENT OF ***SUBJECT R,*** "MADAME RHONDA", SUBJECT P PROCEEDED TO INVESTIGATE.
MADAME
"AT PRECISELY 5:37PM, SUBJECT P DISCOVERED SUBJECT R ***HOLDING THE HAND*** OF SUBJECT F AND FLE INTO WHAT I CAN ONLY DESCRIBE AS A ***JEALOUS RAGE!"***
SHE WAS ONLY ***READING MY PALM!!***
SAVE IT FOR THE JUDGE, FLIPPER...
"AHEM. SUBJECT P THEN PROCEEDED TO INFLICT A ***BODILY ASSAULT*** UPON THE TWO OTHER SUBJECTS...
HAIIII-YAAH!
"AT THAT POINT, THE FULL EXTENT OF SUBJECT R'S ***LARCENOUS ACTIVITIES*** BECAME OBVIOUS!"
MY PURSE!!

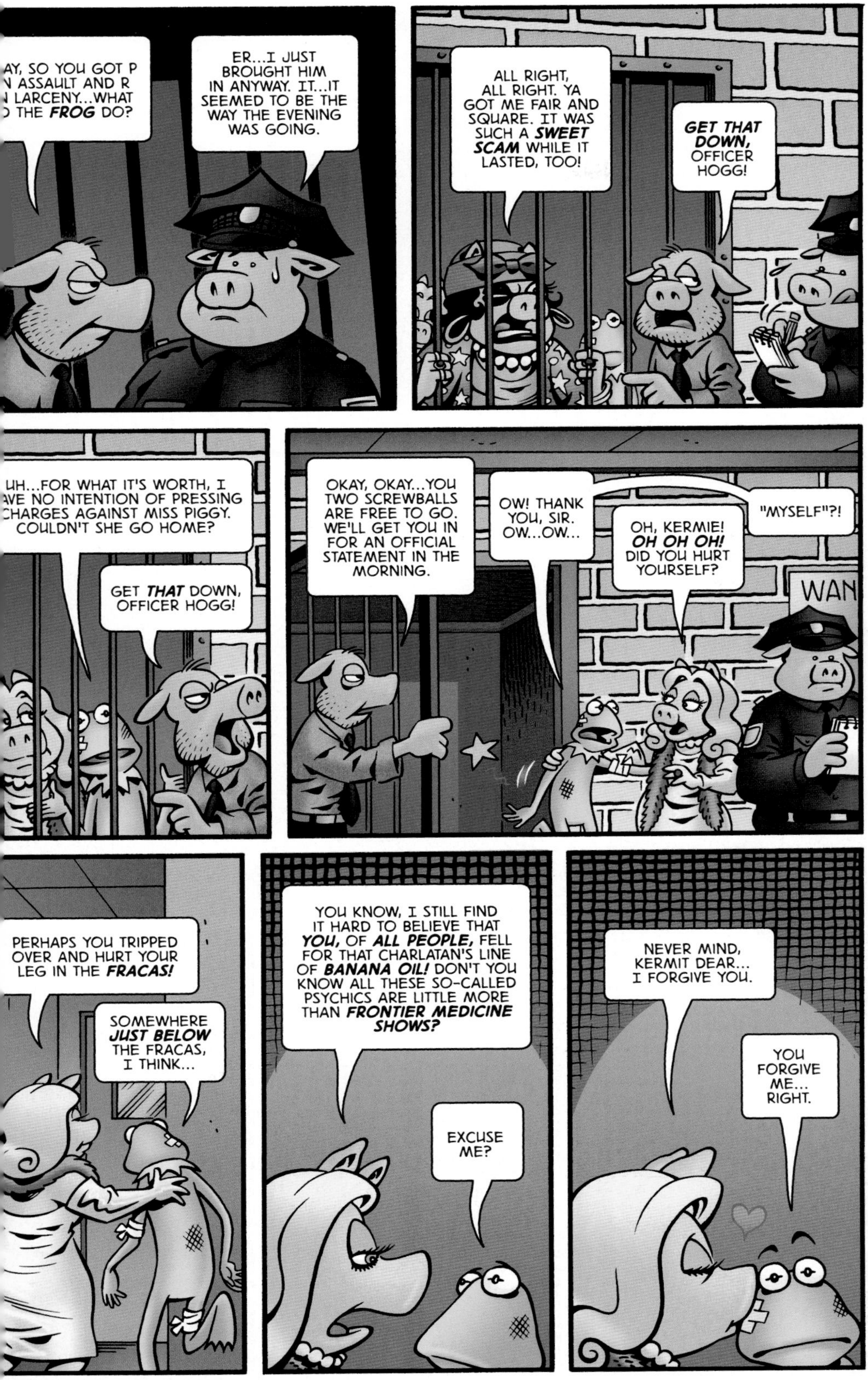
AY, SO YOU GOT P
N ASSAULT AND R
N LARCENY...WHAT
D THE *FROG* DO?
ER...I JUST BROUGHT HIM IN ANYWAY. IT...IT SEEMED TO BE THE WAY THE EVENING WAS GOING.
ALL RIGHT, ALL RIGHT. YA GOT ME FAIR AND SQUARE. IT WAS SUCH A *SWEET SCAM* WHILE IT LASTED, TOO!
GET THAT DOWN, OFFICER HOGG!
UH...FOR WHAT IT'S WORTH, I
AVE NO INTENTION OF PRESSING
CHARGES AGAINST MISS PIGGY.
COULDN'T SHE GO HOME?
GET *THAT* DOWN, OFFICER HOGG!
OKAY, OKAY...YOU TWO SCREWBALLS ARE FREE TO GO. WE'LL GET YOU IN FOR AN OFFICIAL STATEMENT IN THE MORNING.
OW! THANK YOU, SIR. OW...OW...
"MYSELF"?!
OH, KERMIE! *OH OH OH!* DID YOU HURT YOURSELF?
WAN
PERHAPS YOU TRIPPED OVER AND HURT YOUR LEG IN THE *FRACAS!*
SOMEWHERE *JUST BELOW* THE FRACAS, I THINK...
YOU KNOW, I STILL FIND IT HARD TO BELIEVE THAT *YOU, OF ALL PEOPLE,* FELL FOR THAT CHARLATAN'S LINE OF *BANANA OIL!* DON'T YOU KNOW ALL THESE SO-CALLED PSYCHICS ARE LITTLE MORE THAN *FRONTIER MEDICINE SHOWS?*
EXCUSE ME?
NEVER MIND, KERMIT DEAR... I FORGIVE YOU.
YOU FORGIVE ME... RIGHT.

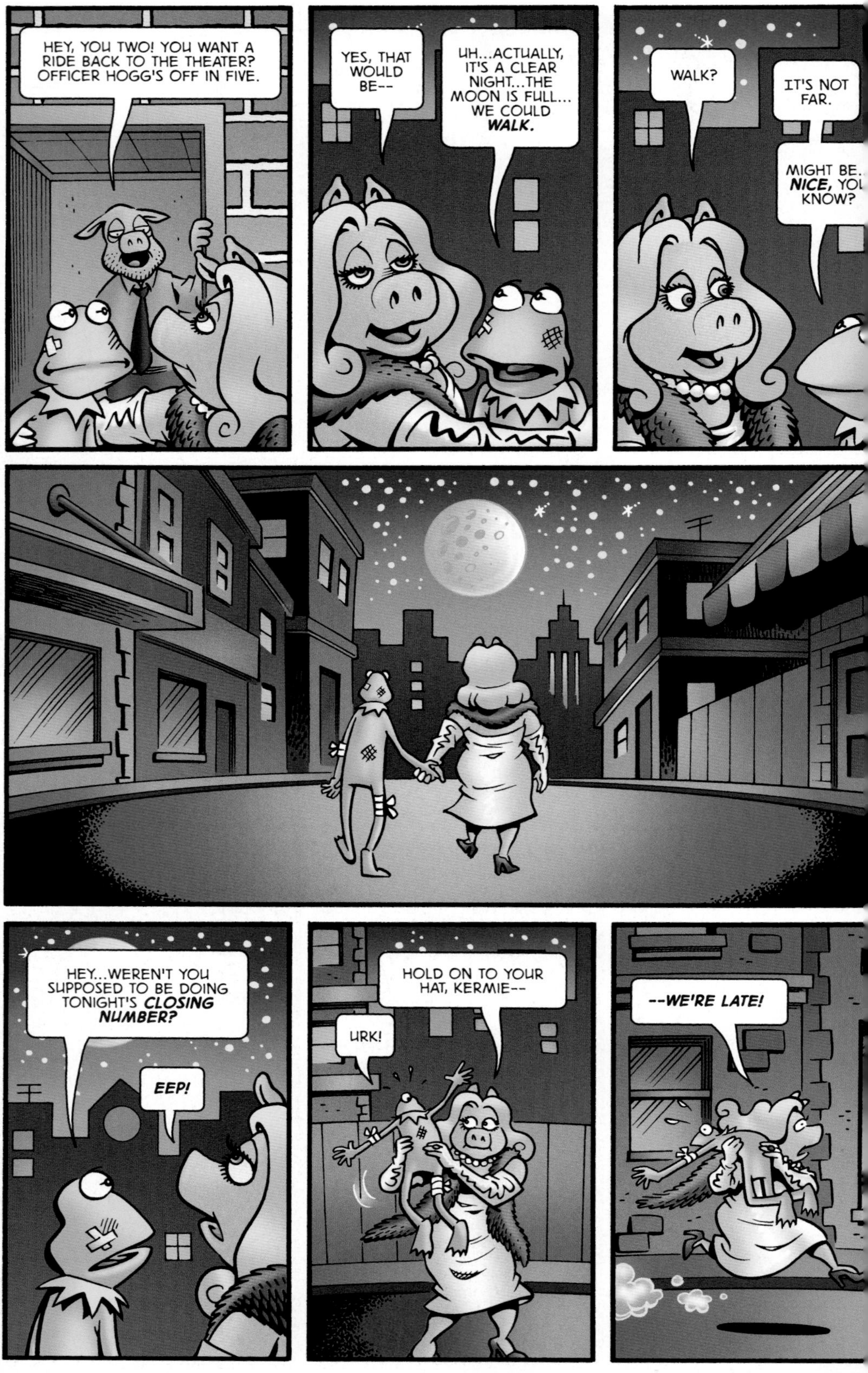
HEY, YOU TWO! YOU WANT A RIDE BACK TO THE THEATER? OFFICER HOGG'S OFF IN FIVE.
YES, THAT WOULD BE--
UH...ACTUALLY, IT'S A CLEAR NIGHT...THE MOON IS FULL... WE COULD WALK.
WALK?
IT'S NOT FAR.
MIGHT BE... NICE, YOU KNOW?
HEY...WEREN'T YOU SUPPOSED TO BE DOING TONIGHT'S CLOSING NUMBER?
EEP!
HOLD ON TO YOUR HAT, KERMIE--
URK!
--WE'RE LATE!

YOU KNOW, YOU'RE GETTING *WAAAY* TOO MANY BANDAGES LATELY. YOU NEED YOUR CHAKRA REALIGNED!

JUST REALIGN MY BONES AND I'LL BE GRATEFUL, JANICE.

HEY, BOSS! CHECK THIS OUT! WE MADE THE *FRONT PAGE!*

SEE?

The Daily Llam

SEVEN YEARS' BAD LU

Bogus psychic Madame Rhonda, alias "Tarot Gertie", alias "Scorpio Lil", alias "Black Claw, Emperor of the Universe", was today sentenced to seven years in prison after the full and dramatic extent of her fraud

came to light in court! Among the people and organizations defrauded of funds amounting to hundreds of thousands of dollars were Ted Ponk's Traveling Flea Circus, the Mercury All-Canine Theater Company, sev friends o

I CAN'T SEE US MENTIONED ANYWHERE.

HERE--RIGHT AT THE BOTTOM, JUST AFTER "GLADYS TERRIBLE'S DONKEY-GROOMING BEAUTY PARLOR".

OH, RIGHT.

LET ME SEE THAT!

I WANT TO READ THAT STORY! I WANT TO READ IT *AGAIN AND AGAIN!* I WANT TO READ IT UNTIL I *WEAR OUT THE PAPER* WITH MY *EYES!*

AH... BE MY GUEST.

IF ANYBODY WANTS ME I'LL BE IN MY DRESSING ROO LAUGHING! *LAUGHING,* DO YO HEAR? AH-HA-HA-HA-HAH

E FIN

THAT WAS *MY* PAPER.

TRUST ME... IT'S HERS NOW.

LATER!

ARIES...SAGITTARIUS... *AH!* HERE WE GO: "YOU WILL MEET A *HANDSOME STRANGER* AND *INHERIT A THOUSAND DOLLARS!"...*

The En

re BOOM! Studios approached me to draw *The Muppet Show* comics, I'd already taken a
 at the characters a couple of years earlier for the magazine *Disney Adventures*. They'd
 running some distinctly off-model Mickey Mouse strips by Glenn McCoy, drawn in a
tchy, underground-comix sort of style, which had proven popular enough that they were
ng to apply a similar treatment to some other Disney property. I'd been doing a bit of
ance illustration for the magazine, and the editors at *Disney Adventures* were familiar
 my other comics work and thought I'd be a good fit for the experiment.

ed up producing a mere 15 pages of material before I got word that *Disney Adventures*
azine had been canceled. Only one page of that initial run saw print in the pages of
 Fozzie Bear strip. The rest were consigned to the dark recesses of some hard drive
ewhere, never to see the light of day... I thought.

hing is, I was inordinately proud of those pages. For the next year, I was aggressively
ving them around to anybody who would look at them, and quite a few people who
ably had no interest in them whatsoever; not with the hopes of finding a publisher or
hing, but simply because I desperately wanted them to be read, by whatever means. And
umably they were circulating behind the scenes at Disney, too, because BOOM! Studios
tually approached me on the strength of those pages and invited me to do a full-length,
tly more on-model comic book version of the show.

me be honest here. The primary impulse for me taking the job on, at least in the
 instance, was to get the *Disney Adventures* pages into print somehow. It seemed to
that there would be a much greater chance of them finally being published if I were
ssociate myself with the Muppets for a few months longer and get enough material
ther for a book. Put the *Disney Adventures* in the back as a bonus feature and voilà!
ion accomplished! And the Muppets and I would be done with one another.

sn't quite worked out that way. The BOOM! Studios *Muppet Show* comic has picked up
rrible momentum of its own and I hope to be associated with it for a while yet. It's been
 of the most satisfying projects of my professional life, fitting my own interests and
sibilities like some crazy three-fingered glove. But I'm still thrilled to have my original
pet Show material presented to the world in its entirety, in full colour and without me
ng to buy anybody a drink, for the very first time. This is the tiny, ugly baby that would
tually grow up to be the eight foot gorilla you hold in your hands today. Enjoy.

er Langridge
don, July 2009

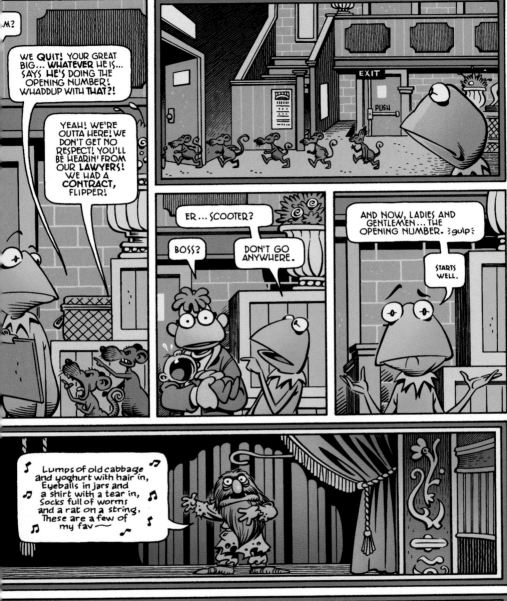

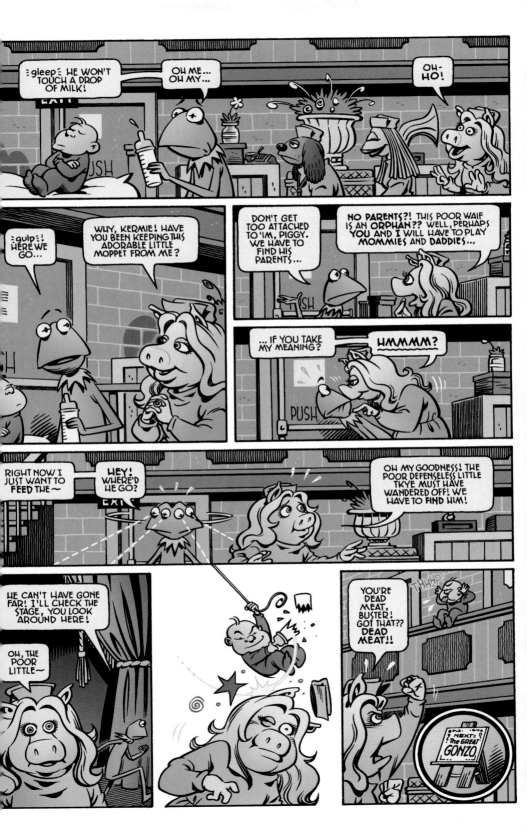

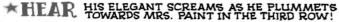

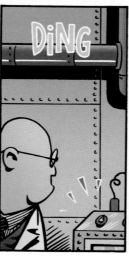

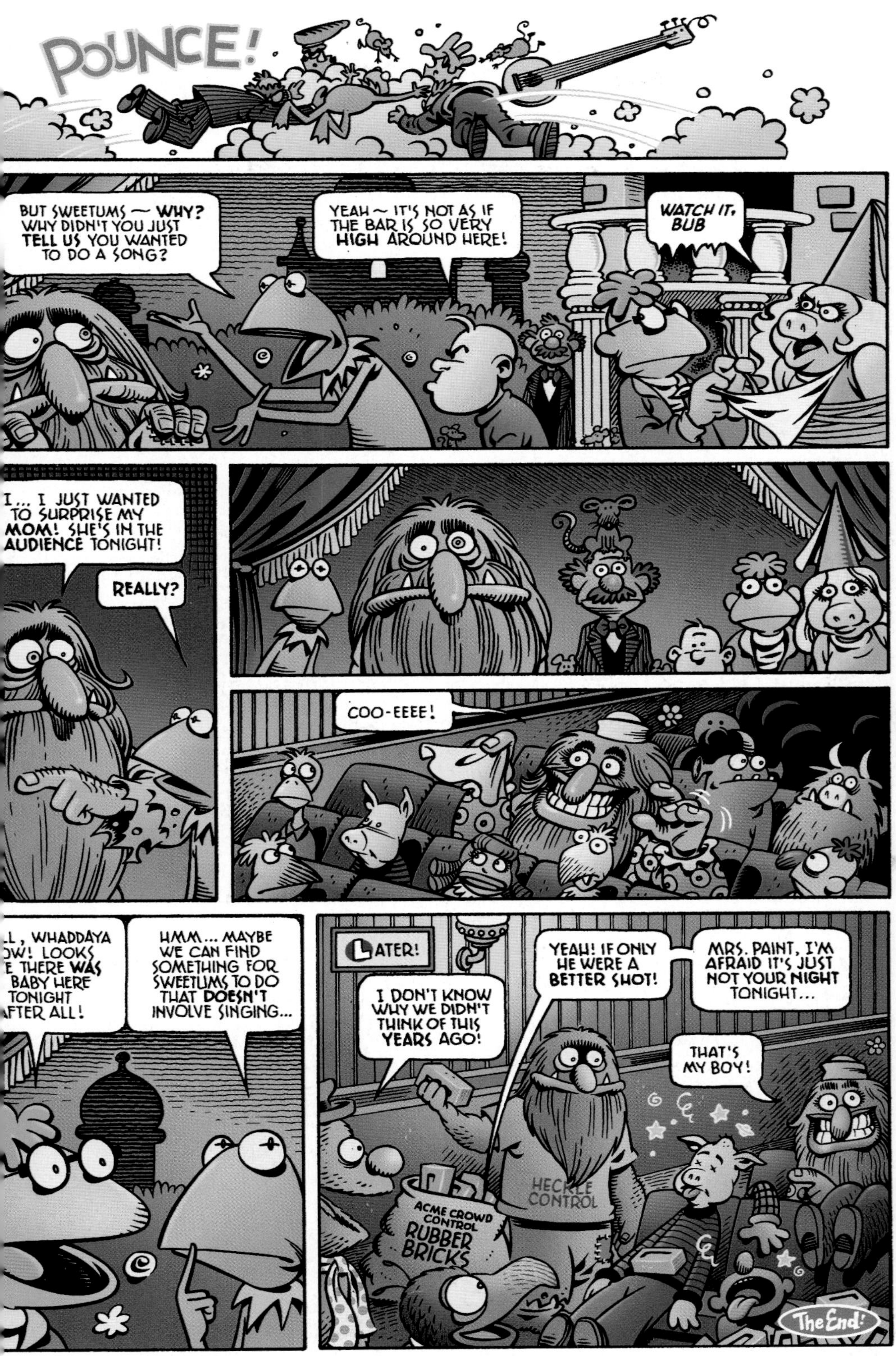
POUNCE!
BUT SWEETUMS — WHY? WHY DIDN'T YOU JUST TELL US YOU WANTED TO DO A SONG?
YEAH ~ IT'S NOT AS IF THE BAR IS SO VERY HIGH AROUND HERE!
WATCH IT, BUB
I... I JUST WANTED TO SURPRISE MY MOM! SHE'S IN THE AUDIENCE TONIGHT!
REALLY?
COO-EEEE!
LL, WHADDAYA OW! LOOKS E THERE WAS BABY HERE TONIGHT FTER ALL!
HMM... MAYBE WE CAN FIND SOMETHING FOR SWEETUMS TO DO THAT DOESN'T INVOLVE SINGING...
LATER!
I DON'T KNOW WHY WE DIDN'T THINK OF THIS YEARS AGO!
YEAH! IF ONLY HE WERE A BETTER SHOT!
MRS. PAINT, I'M AFRAID IT'S JUST NOT YOUR NIGHT TONIGHT...
THAT'S MY BOY!
HECKLE CONTROL
ACME CROWD CONTROL RUBBER BRICKS
The End!

LADIES and GENTLEMEN! It's that Master of Mirth... BOYS and GIRLS! That Guru of Gags... FOZZIE BEAR!

A FUNNY BEAR

A DISMAL PAIR

A TALENT RARE

AN ICY STARE

A SUDDEN FLARE

LIFE'S SO UNFAIR